Also by J.H. Bográn

Treasure Hunt

FIREFALL

J.H. BOGRÁN

12/2/13

To Tim!

Well, I guess this can be considered my lost set of documents!

Jose Rene Bográn

Rebel ePublishers
Detroit New York London Johannesburg

Rebel ePublishers
Detroit, Michigan 48223

Firefall
© 2013 by J.H. Bográn

ISBN-13: 978-0615883151
ISBN-10: 061588315X

Cover design by *Literra Design*, *www.litteradesigns.com*
Interior design by *Caryatid Design*

ACKNOWLEDGEMENTS

In a novel that took me as long to write as this one, the road to publication was filled with people whose insights made this story a far better one than the silly plot points I jotted down back in 2006.

The early readers who commented, made me see the reason, and helped ground the story were Tami Parrington, Elaine Breault, Marge Conrad, Reese Greer, Douglas Brown and Gina Fava.

The charming and professional people at Hotel Villas Telamar who let me snoop around, camera in hand, throughout the hotels premises: Maira Morillo, Ana Chicas, Tania Chavarría, Reyna Gomez and Victor Mendoza.

Jim Thompson, Aleyda and Oscar Chavarría helped me with information regarding Texas in general and Dallas in particular.

When it came to insurance fraud and odd cases, I turned to José Fuentes and Roy Reyes.

The torture scene near the end would not have been as detailed if not for the coffee and conversation I held with Mario Berríos and Bladimir Burgos.

From Backspace online Forum, where I bored people with chapter excerpts and dumb questions, I specially have to thank Karen Dionne, Chris Graham, Loretta, Lisa, Irene, Exeye, Ian, Helen, Bonnie, Gavin, Ly, Anne, Daryl, Gregg, Sara, Lauren, Richard, Maggie, Chris, JV, Melissa, Inge, Keith and Catcher.

To my family who allowed me some time to sneak

away and plot, jot & rewrite.

At Rebel ePublishers I've had the pleasure to work with wonderful professionals like Jayne Southern, EJ Knapp, Rachel Cole among others. To them, my eternal gratitude!

A special thanks to Catherine Lea, you gave me Firefall!

To every man and woman who has the courage to walk into a fire for reasons above and beyond a paycheck.

CHAPTER ONE

NEW YORK CITY, NEW YORK

It's easy to be reborn from the ashes. The only catch is, you have to die first.

Today Sebastian Martin turned thirty-nine and to celebrate, his older brother, James, had decided dinner in a fancy restaurant would be the best gift.

"Good evening Mr. Martin. Reservation for three?" the hostess greeted James.

Damn! She knows him by name, Sebastian thought. James's practice as a therapist must be going well if he can afford fancy restaurants – wait, she said table for three. "I thought Christine wasn't coming," Sebastian said.

James smiled at the young woman, then turned to Sebastian. After lowering his eyes as if searching for the answer on the floor, he said, "She isn't. PTA meeting."

"Then?"

Sebastian hadn't stepped out of his apartment much in the last six months. Without Kelly and Joshua, he didn't see the point.

"Uncle Mike."

An invitation out of the blue from his brother, Christine bowing out – of course she would, almost all of their conversations ended in an argument – and now, their only living relative comes to New York all the way from Texas. Sebastian smelled a trap.

The hostess led the way to the table. Sebastian gave

one last look at the door, his escape route. This was his last chance to run away from whatever his relatives had in store for him. As a firefighter for the FDNY, he had no fear about walking into a blazing building, but entering a safe restaurant for a meal with his family drained the last ounce of his self-discipline.

James stopped and turned, as if sensing Sebastian's indecision. Even at fifteen feet away, James's green eyes projected a look like laser beams.

Sebastian felt the burn, his skin tingled. With his last window of opportunity gone, he sighed and caught up with James.

The tantalizing aromas of meat, sauces and assorted condiments, bombarded Sebastian. His stomach churned. He hadn't realized he was hungry. The last full meal was the McDonald's Dollar Menu he had paid the neighbor's kid to buy for him. Before leaving home, he had picked up the crumpled receipt from the floor and checked the date: two days ago. Where had yesterday gone?

A waiter approached the table. "Can we offer you something to drink?"

"Vodka tonic," said Sebastian at once.

James stared. Sebastian met his gaze with a defiant look and sat down. Sebastian noticed that James either overlooked or ignored the brotherly stare-down contest. The waiter just stood there, with that perky smile, looking but not really seeing.

"The same for me." James said, with a forced smile.

The waiter nodded and left.

"How did you find this place?"

"Oh, a patient of mine recommended it. Trust me, you'll love it."

Their drinks arrived. Sebastian raised his crystal glass to propose a toast. "To you, big brother," he said and gulped half the contents before he placed the glass back on the table.

James's jaw dropped. Even at this age, annoying him was very easy; it was almost no fun at all. Almost.

When James finished his first drink, and Sebastian his third, Uncle Mike arrived. The gray silk suit he wore looked expensive. He must have visited Savile Row again. The striking pink tie with the Windsor knot over a deep blue shirt gave him a debonair look. His jet-black hair was combed straight back and kept in place by what must have been great amounts of hair gel. James stood to greet him, but had to wait as Sebastian endured a prolonged embrace.

Uncle Mike lived in Dallas and had a big case that had made it impossible for him to come to Kelly and Joshua's funeral. Indeed, this was the first time he'd seen Sebastian since their deaths.

After he sat down, he adjusted his shirt cuffs with his manicured hands. The initialed gold cufflinks shone under the light. He looked more like a slick Hollywood star than an accomplished mid-fifties lawyer.

At the sight of the last chair occupied, the waiter approached again. "Ready to order?"

Sebastian hated how waiters hovered around the table like UFOs and landed on the patrons at the first opportunity. "Damn it, he just parked his butt on the seat," he said.

The waiter fidgeted with obvious embarrassment. Sebastian took another sip of his drink, then chewed the ice cube he had left behind.

"I can come back later if you prefer."

"No need. I'll have the Lobster Thermidor." Uncle Mike did not even glance at the menu. "I've tried it before."

"The same for me." Sebastian closed his menu. "And bring me another round."

"Krieger's cut, medium rare," said James. "I like the

way the chef prepares this plate, as spicy as a pepper steak, but not covered with the typical buttery sauce."

"Since when did you become a gourmet?" Sebastian said.

James ignored the jibe and took a sip of his drink. It seemed two could play that game.

"So, you're back putting out fires?" Uncle Mike said to Sebastian.

"Not yet."

"How long has it been?"

"He's been on paid leave for six months now," James said.

"Guys, I thought this was a birthday dinner. It feels more like a cross examination!" Sebastian eyed Uncle Mike and added, "Besides which, James, I can answer for myself, thank you."

"Nonsense." The lawyer didn't even flinch or trade a look with James. "On the contrary, we've got a job offer for you."

Damn, he's good! went through Sebastian's mind.

"I have a job."

"Seb, I love you, but do you think it's fair for the Fire Department to keep you on the payroll if you're not working?" said James.

Sebastian lowered his gaze. It was a cheap shot. Bastard.

"Have they said anything?" Sebastian knew it was lame, but he couldn't think of any other defense.

"Of course they wouldn't. You know that!" James said. "I talked to Doctor Richards. We went to school together. He risked confiding in me, as I'm your next of kin. He didn't reveal any secrets, but says you're not up for it anymore. He knows you have the skills but lost the will and inclination."

"Will?" Sebastian scoffed, "I've lost my inclination? That's it? I lost my *family*!" His fist pounded on the table causing the plates, glasses and assorted knives and forks to jump and rattle. People at the next table raised eyebrows in their direction.

The moment he'd woken up with James sitting by his bed and offering a dinner invitation, he'd known this little get-together meant trouble. He wished he'd taken back James's key to the apartment.

"Seb," Uncle Mike said, "I do have a job offer. It is a good opportunity and it's right for you." The tone was neutral, casual. Like the opening statement before a jury.

"Out of curiosity, what is it?" Sebastian spoke through clenched teeth.

"Remember my friend, Roger Simmons?"

"He's the accountant who sat next to you when they hijacked that airliner back in the seventies."

Sebastian remembered the whole story, entrenched as it was in the family history. The jet had been held to ransom, midair. Once on the ground and under threat of blowing everybody up, the perpetrator forced Uncle Mike and Roger Simmons to help. As kids, James and Sebastian had made their uncle retell the story and explain how they had served as human shields to the bad guy as they crossed over the landing field to a plane on the next ramp. Sebastian in particular had wanted to hear the story again and again.

"Yes, but he's more than an accountant now. He heads an investigation office for a major insurance company."

"Private investigator?" Sebastian's eyebrow shot up.

"Well, not exactly." Uncle Mike spoke with assurance, in his element. "When you file a claim saying a Picasso was stolen from your living room, they don't just write a check. They check you out, consult the police, and look over your finances. You know, make sure it's not hidden in the garage."

"Sounds great," said Sebastian, smiling. He knew James would know this was his way of saying "Fuck you!"

"The money's not bad either," added Mike. It seemed the irony of Sebastian's comment was lost on him.

"Speaking of money, Uncle Mike, I found this letter on Seb's dresser." James fished out a sealed envelope from his breast pocket and slid it over the table. "Take a look."

A glimpse at the logo on the envelope was all it took for Sebastian's face to suffuse with anger. The sound of his fist banging on the table muffled the sound of the curse he uttered. "How dare you! That's my mail, you dirty sneaking little brat! You can go to jail for this."

Mike's hand froze over the envelope.

"Relax, Sebastian. Given your current behavior, I can have you committed and order your mail to be screened. As it is, I'm just saving paperwork." James held Sebastian's gaze for a full minute.

Mike took and opened the envelope. After he skimmed over the content, he scoffed, breaking the concentration of the stare-down. "Those bastards!"

"What is it?" James turned to Uncle Mike.

Defeating his older brother in a stare-down was no small achievement. Sebastian celebrated with another gulp of the vodka tonic.

"They're offering two million dollars to compensate for Kelly and Joshua. Only catch is, you have to sign an affidavit stating the matter is finalized so you can't sue them later."

James whispered, "Two million is not bad."

Sebastian snorted.

Mike turned to Sebastian. "Not bad? You've got to be kidding me! I'd sue their asses for five mil each, at least. Let me go after these a-holes for you."

"You can get me five million for Kelly, and another five million for Joshua?"

6

Uncle Mike nodded, a confident smirk on his face. "Okay, sounds great. Now, do you think you can bring Kelly and Joshua back to life with that money?" Sebastian's eyes bulged, grief and rage etched on his face. He watched Mike's face go blank with astonishment as he realized the crass mistake he had made in bringing money into the equation.

Sebastian understood his uncle's point of view; he was a lawyer; obtaining multi-million dollar settlements from big corporations was what he did every day. Sebastian on the other hand, always worked in the field of saving lives with the New York Fire Department. He'd work just as hard to save a mansion or a ramshackle shack. He dealt in human lives, not currency.

"Look, we understand," James said, obviously eager to patch up things. "We cared about them too." He paused until Sebastian's breathing returned to normal. "We are here because we care about you. You are all we have left of that wonderful little family."

"Sometimes it's too much to bear. The notion that I will never see them again is ..." His voice broke. Sebastian grabbed his glass and gulped down the vodka.

"We're all worried about you and I can't let you drink yourself to the grave." James lowered his eyes as if the luster on the silverware in front of him demanded his attention.

Another awkward silence descended. The waiter brought their order. Sebastian ate, but he had no appetite and it was clear his companions felt the same. The only sound was the occasional fork scraping on the plate.

"Is there an interview?" Sebastian's voice was flat and even, his anger dissipated.

"Yes." Mike looked relieved. "In Dallas. I know you won't fly there, so I had my secretary print out driving directions. It's a twenty-two hour trip." He pulled out two folded sheets and passed them across.

"Texas, huh?" Sebastian scanned the printed road maps.

"Yes. Brenda will love to have you home," Uncle Mike reassured him.

"Thank your wife for me. I'll let you know if I go," said Sebastian, polite and noncommittal. He folded the pages and pocketed them.

CHAPTER TWO

CORTÉS, HONDURAS

Howard Gonzales glanced at the bright blue Caribbean peeking through the breaks in the dense vegetation. The single lane blacktop road snaked around the mountains heading north. The air that blew in through the window and sunroof smelled of salt and pine.

He checked the rearview mirror. His four companions were following at a safe distance. He'd chosen to ride in the car because of its stereo system. His over-scratched, illegally downloaded mp3 CD sounded like the original from his favorite Tex-Mex band.

He burped and tasted onion. Fried fish, topped with pickled onions, and plantain chips on the side was Omoa's most popular dish, but the reflux could kill you.

The town was thirty minutes from San Pedro Sula on the same coastline road that connected to Guatemala. On weekends, it would be crowded with people enjoying a day at the white-sand beach, and others who would drive there just for lunch.

His right arm itched. Howard had felt it burning from the scorching sun shining amidst the odd-shaped white clouds. He pushed a button and the sunroof slid shut.

He ran a small operation compared with other gangs stealing cars in the country. His team consisted of five people; Pablo, Gregorio and Manuel were mechanics capable of taking a car apart in record time; Marcos, his second in command, ran the mechanics with the intensity of a drill sergeant. He taught them how to shoot and he planned all the 'acquisitions.' He would change tactics and procedures as he saw fit, depending on the target.

Gregorio was an expert at hot-wiring cars, so Marcos would always take him when they targeted stationary vehicles, in particular from outside bars, when speed was of the essence. The green car Howard was driving was one such case.

Pablo and Manuel had the social grace of hippos; their intimidating physiques were useful for straightforward carjacks, where unsuspecting car owners left the engine running while they opened the garage door.

The last member was the key to the success of his operation. Carlos was a hacker and forger whose abilities were best utilized off the field. He helped to steal cars from the luxury of a plush chair in front of a computer.

An armed guard signaled Howard to stop when he approached the border between Honduras and Guatemala. "Good afternoon," he said.

The guard gave an almost imperceptible nod in reply, looked at the car, frowned, and read from his clipboard.

As an expert trained in assault, Howard marveled at the ease with which they could take down this place. The guard had a heavy, Cold War-era rifle hanging from his shoulder and on top of that, his hands were busy with a clipboard. He estimated the guard's response time would be five seconds too late. Not even a fighting chance.

"Is this your car?" The guard's voice sounded like a cross between a bark and a grunt.

"Yes, it is."

"Registration and ID." The guard held out one hand.

This was the moment of truth. Even after a couple of years of monthly trips, Howard tensed when crossing the border. He pulled out his ID. Nicaraguan by birth, Howard had acquired Honduran citizenship when he married a local and kept it after his divorce.

The car registration card was barely thicker than regular paper. Made on flimsy cream-colored cardboard, it had pre-printed frames in colors that changed every year.

This year the chosen color was brown. The card listed information about the vehicle and the legal owner: chassis number, engine serial number, plate number and the total amount of tax due each year; the card doubled as the receipt, with a bank stamp and teller signature on the back.

The cards were the reason he paid Carlos so well. An expert graphic artist, Carlos duplicated and printed new registration cards, each with the name of the driver taking the stolen vehicle across the border.

If you were not the owner, Honduras law demanded a special notarized permit to allow the car out of the country. If the registration showed the name of the driver, then all the frontier guard did was take a perfunctory look and let the car pass.

The guard studied both documents. Howard held his breath. The guard looked down on his clipboard. One eternal minute later, the guard handed him the documents and waved him on without another word.

Another guard lowered the rope that blocked the way. Howard listened to the familiar *thu-thump* as he drove over the thick rope. He had made it, yet again. Now he was in no-man's land, an area of about two miles between both countries.

A one-story building that housed the immigration offices, sat about a block after the frontier rope barrier. Howard parked the car and stepped out. He walked toward one of the bank teller-like windows, his ID in hand.

As of 2003, the need for natives of Guatemala, El Salvador, Nicaragua and Honduras, referred to as the C-4, to use passports to cross the border by land, sea or air had been abolished. Since then, the ID card was sufficient.

Howard held up his card to the immigration officer sitting inside. The man gave it a cursory look and dismissed him. Howard returned to his car and drove away.

About a mile down the road, another thick rope blocked the road but the guards lowered it without bothering about documentation. Howard accelerated and he and the stolen car entered Guatemala.

Five miles behind him, Carlos rode with Marcos in a Dodge Caravan. Howard reveled in Marcos's animosity toward Carlos. Deep down, he deemed it safer that they hated each other so much. That way, it would keep them from plotting against him.

The road was black asphalt with the international white stripe in the middle. Banana plantations lined both sides of the road; plastic bags wrapped around the fruit created mini-greenhouses to accelerate the ripening process.

A few minutes later, his cellular phone beeped once. It sounded like a sonar system on a submarine. He read the message: Marcos and Carlos had made it across the border.

He expected to receive similar text messages within the next ten or twenty minutes. He marveled how new technology made his job easier. His cell beeped again, this time Manuel checked in. Pablo's text message followed it.

The last text message from Gregorio made him stomp on the brake.

Chapter Three

Border Station, Honduras

Marcos parked the Dodge Caravan in front of the Honduran immigration building.

"You know, most of our population is a mixture of Spanish and natives, and even blacks. I mean, we're not even all white, but we sure are damn racists," Carlos said.

"What do you mean?"

"Look at this. They let all of us through except the one black dude."

Marcos's fingers tightened around the steering wheel. Carlos could pick the worst occasions to make the most stupid and trivial comments but then, everything he said was dumb in Marcos's opinion.

"You plan to just walk in there and get Gregorio out?"

Marcos hated Carlos's condescending tone. "In short, yes," he snapped and stepped out of the car.

"What do I do?"

Marcos leaned through the open window and said, "You can go. I'll ride with Gregorio."

"Do you think you will get him off?"

"Yes."

"Can I help?"

Marcos shook his head. "You stick to your computer and let me do the real man's work."

He moved away from the car and walked toward the building. He heard the engine noise fading as Carlos drove away. A smile crossed his face; having the last word pleased

Marcos, even if it was a small victory.

He had belittled Carlos with confidence, but now, alone and about to enter the immigration building, doubts assailed him. He did not know why the guards had detained Gregorio, and worse, he didn't know if the car was still here. It should be, it had only been fifteen minutes. Just the time it took to notify Howard and read the simple text reply: SOLVE IT.

Looking at the rectangular one-story building and the two windows for immigration services, Marcos knew Gregorio would not be there. He went to the right where a corridor went all the way to the back. He followed it, found a large parking lot on the other side, and realized there were two buildings: the front one with the immigration booths and a second in the back, two-stories high and painted in the same off-white color.

Two cars were parked in the street-wide space between the buildings. One of them was the blue Hyundai Gregorio had been driving. With no guard in sight, he walked over to the car and tried the door: locked. He turned his gaze back to the building and saw a sign saying *Dirección Ejecutiva de Ingresos*, DEI or Executive Board of Income. The Board was the government agency that issued car registrations. Marcos figured that if Carlos had screwed up with the ID card, the DEI was the most likely place where they'd detain his black mechanic.

He approached the building and doing his best to project a casual demeanor, looked through the open window. Four desks occupied most of the space. Paired against opposite sides of the room, leaving space between them, Gregorio sat at the farthest desk with his hands cuffed to the back of a chair.

He went in. "Gregorio, what happened?"

Gregorio looked relieved to see him. "The guards at the gate said they couldn't believe I'd own such a nice new car."

"Racist bastards!"

14

"After they brought me here, the officer ran the car's chassis number on his computer and it came up as stolen."

Marcos knew Carlos could fake the IDs but wasn't skilled enough to hack into the system and change the official registration. "Where's the officer now?"

"He said he was hungry, took the money from my wallet, and went out." He gave a wry smile. "He said he'd try to bring me a drink with the spare change."

"Damn!" Marcos tried to shake off his anger. He needed to keep his wits about him.

Howard kept telling him he had to manage his anger better and warned him he'd regret hasty decisions. Marcos would counter that his instincts, more often than not, were right. This was the time, he figured, to act on instinct.

He locked the door and walked over to the desk. He checked Gregorio's restraints and turned to the desk to look for something useful to pick the handcuffs. He spotted a small plastic cup filled with assorted paperclips. He took one of the bigger ones.

"Keep an eye on the window."

Gregorio nodded.

Marcos straightened one end of the clip and introduced it into the lock, jiggling it around. "Where's the car key?"

"Took it with him."

He had planned to free Gregorio and get the hell out of there, but it seemed fate had other plans. "We'll have to find the bastard after all."

He twisted the paperclip again, and with a click, the cuff opened. Without wasting time, he turned to work on the other one and finished it faster.

"Tell me what he looks like then go wait by the car. Don't let anybody see you."

Gregorio described the officer and left.

Marcos went out of the building and turned right, back into the Honduran side. A shack painted with the striking colors of a popular soft drink stood nearby, selling inexpen-

15

sive local food. Plastic tables and chairs occupied the front decking under zinc roofing. They served the food through a window from the kitchen on the far side.

He stepped onto the wooden deck, looking at the patrons sitting in groups of two and three. Except one. He recognized the DEI white cotton uniform shirt and black pants. The shirt strained against the round belly. A badge on the left chest pocket provided the final confirmation. The other three chairs at the square table were empty. The officer hunched over the table wolfing down *pollo con tajadas*, fried chicken and fried banana chips with chopped cabbage, topped with a dark red tomato sauce.

Marcos had planned to intercept the guard when he returned to the office but he could not stand around and wait there, he would be too conspicuous; he had to blend in with the crowd. Approaching the window, he ordered a *baleada*, Honduras's best-known typical food, a flour tortilla folded in half and filled with refried beans, butter, and cheese. Variants included avocados, scrambled eggs and even sausages. With his hunger for deliverance greater than for food, Marcos added none of the extras.

The girl inside prepared his order in less than a minute. He took the disposable plate and went to a table.

"Excuse me, do you mind if I sit here? Place is crowded." He had to speak loud enough to combat the blasting Latin music from the radio.

The guard looked up, chewing a chunk of his *pollo*, and nodded.

Marcos sat down and wondered should the guy choke on a chicken bone, whether it would be what people referred to as poetic justice.

Marcos pulled his sticking shirt off his back not knowing if his sweating was because of the hot weather or his apprehension. The knots in his stomach tilted the scale to the latter. He couldn't eat, so he sipped his soda instead.

The DEI officer wasted no time in idle conversation with

a stranger. After he ate the last chip, he licked the remains of the sauce off his fingers. Then he finished his drink in one long suck of the straw. The man thumped on his chest, as if shaking loose a piece of food stuck in his esophagus, his mouth closed all the time.

Shame, Marcos thought, belching in my face would have provided an excuse to attack him in public. Bar brawls had started for much less than that.

The official shifted his position on the chair. He seemed to want to pull up a leg to cross it but his belly didn't allow for the necessary physical space to accomplish it.

"Why aren't you eating?" The guard looked at Marcos's untouched *baleada*. "Nothing tastes worse than cold fried beans."

"Too hot." Marcos thought the man might ask for his food if he said he'd lost his appetite.

"Ah."

Marcos forced himself to take a bite and chew. When he swallowed, he felt sick. He knew he should not eat before a kill.

The man looked bored but made no further attempt to converse.

Marcos had no detailed plan of how to deal with the guard. His only objective was the key. He was running on instinct.

Marcos knew his limitations. He was not a con artist but a lethal weapon, trained by the military and now serving under Howard Gonzales again. Together they had experienced their share of near-fatal screw-up missions. Now they stole cars, sold them, and made a decent amount of money.

The DEI officer rose from the chair and left without the courtesy of a nod goodbye. The floorboards creaked with every step of his heavy boots until he stepped down and out of the shack.

Marcos counted to twenty and went out leaving the half-eaten food on the table.

The man had a slow gait, rocking like a huge vessel anchored on open waters. Marcos followed from five paces behind. The man reached his office while Marcos counted on the element of surprise at not finding the prisoner cuffed to the chair. Instead, the man surprised Marcos by turning into the men's room.

Marcos made sure nobody was around as he went in. The restroom was no bigger than three meters by three meters. The right wall held the wash-hand basin, a white urinal next to it and a booth at the far end to provide some privacy. The odors and sounds left no doubt of what was happening inside.

Marcos was alone with the revenue officer. His tennis shoes squeaked on the tile floor as he approached the basin to wash his hands. He was not concerned with fingerprints; they wouldn't show on any database. The late KGB had burned off his prints from his fingers when he first began to do their dirty deeds. He looked into the sad eyes gazing back at him from the mirror. It was time.

He removed his sneakers and placed them behind the door. Silence rewarded him as he tiptoed in his socks.

He positioned himself so the man could not see his feet from under the door of the booth and inspected the hinges, ascertaining the door opened inward. Marcos stood poised like a statue, ready like a coiled spring, waiting for the man to emerge.

The guard came out and as planned, surprise registered on his face. Marcos used his right thumb to strike the spot where the man's sternum met with the beginning of his round belly. The man gasped. Another rapid jab to his windpipe. Marcos entered the booth in time to catch the limp body. Just then, he heard the doorknob turning. He'd forgotten to lock the restroom door. He pushed and closed the cubicle door with his heel.

The *tap-tap* of footsteps, different from his squeaking tennis shoes, indicated the new arrival wore dress shoes or boots. A fly unzipped, followed by a steady flow.

The DEI guy stirred. Marcos moved to strangle him with one hand while covering his mouth with the other, but too late, the man gave a soft groan.

"Hey, Juan, is that you?"

Marcos's heartbeat increased for the first time since he heard the news about Gregorio. He clenched his teeth and emitted a low but sustained grunt as if his bowels were giving him trouble.

"Okay, I can hear you're busy." The stranger rushed out without even washing his hands.

Marcos sighed with relief or at least, he tried to. He was in good shape for someone in his mid-thirties, but holding the fat limp bastard was taxing. He eased the body to the floor and locked the restroom door.

Returning to the cubicle, he removed the dark leather belt. Out of curiosity, Marcos checked for the size: 48. Stepping on the toilet seat, he reached the low ceiling and tied the belt to one of the iron beams supporting the zinc roof. Then the hard part. Heaving and sweating, he pulled up the body and tied it by the neck.

He exited the booth and turned to see his work, his head tilted in mock appreciation. The fat man hung from the ceiling and gently swung like a pendulum. If he'd done it right, Marcos felt sure the police would dismiss it as a suicide. A cynical smile crossed his face as he realized Gregorio had paid for the officer's last supper.

Gregorio! He'd still be by the car.

He patted down the body, found a wallet, some money, a Swiss Army knife, a pack of cigarettes and matches. He found everything but the damn car key.

Had he killed the wrong man?

Gregorio had described him in detail: the black hair, the white shirt and black pants, the stubs of a beard, and of course, the body shape.

It didn't make sense. He took a deep breath to calm

19

down. Assuming he had the right person, Marcos deduced the key must be somewhere in the office. He grabbed his shoes and rushed out, careful to lock the door again and pocket the key, to delay the discovery of the body for as long as possible.

Returning to the office, he searched the desktop and found nothing. He opened all the drawers with the same result. He looked around; he even knelt down to see if the guard had unwittingly dropped the keys on the floor. He checked the other desks for good measure but found nothing. He left, feeling cheated by fate, and found Gregorio sitting by the car.

"Can you wire the car?" Marcos asked.

Gregorio opened his mouth but closed it again as if he had thought better of it. He sighed and then said, "Yes, but I need the stick."

Marcos groaned. To prevent theft, recent model car keys incorporated a coded chip in the base. You could circumvent the need of the key, but without the electronic code, the engine would not turn. The stick was a short cylindrical object, hence the name, that contained a transmitter. The transmitter could be programmed to emit a signal that the car computer would recognize. Carlos was an expert in programming the stick.

"I bet Carlos brought one in his car. Why don't you call him?"

In frustration, Marcos kicked one of the tires of the car. He had felt so high and mighty in sending Carlos off and now he had to call him back. Oh, how the bastard would enjoy that!

His pride proved harder to chew than the tortilla and beans. With great reluctance, he pulled out his cell phone and dialed.

CHAPTER FOUR

SAN PEDRO SULA, HONDURAS

Despite the humidity and heat, Gustavo Fonseca loved living in San Pedro Sula. He still had a soft spot for Tegucigalpa, but came to live here after his discharge from the Honduras Armed Forces.

He turned the knob and pushed open the heavy door into his rented office. A fine line of sweat broke from his wide forehead as he stepped in. Gustavo switched the lights on after closing the door. He walked past his desk, dropped his bulky black day planner, which contained his 9mm ASP handgun in a concealed zipped compartment.

He took a small remote control from his desktop and pushed a button. The air conditioner emitted a soft rumble.

After powering up his Dell desktop, he went to the other side of the office. A row of four black metal three-drawer-cabinets stood against the wall. They doubled as a table with glass resting on top. The soft gurgle of the automatic coffee maker filled the room with the sweet scent of the aromatic blend, a domestic brand he had discovered a few years back. Gustavo worked and lived on coffee. Next to the machine sat a tray holding several inverted mugs. He took his own, the tallest one, red with computer motifs. He didn't feel quite in office mode until he had the warm ceramic in his hand.

By the time he'd prepared his fuel – black with a single spoon of sugar – and returned to his desk, the computer had finished loading. He sat on his swivel chair, and placed his mug in the holder that kept his brew hot. He opened his e-mail box and let out a whistle when he noticed the number of incoming messages: one hundred eight.

He scanned the subject lines one by one. Most were news flashes from several servers he subscribed to, others were from the U.S. insurance companies that kept him on retainer.

His biggest account was Real American Insurance Company. He did not sell policies for them; his duties were more investigative. After five years in this line of work, it still amazed him to discover insurance fraud was so prevalent companies were forced to hire investigators like him to find out if they really had to pay. Every time a reimbursement report seemed shady or out of range, he worked for a flat rate per case, but earned a commission if he proved any intention to defraud on the policyholder's part.

The phone rang, breaking his concentration. He pushed the speaker button.

"*Buenos Días.*"

"*Hola,* Gustavo. How are you?"

"Hello, Mr. Simmons. What can I do for you?" He switched to accented but good English.

"You sound so far away. Did you put me on the damn speaker again?" Simmons sounded annoyed.

Gustavo grimaced and picked up the receiver. "Sorry, I forgot you hate that," he mumbled in apology.

"No problem. I know you like to hold your Java mug when you're on the phone." It amused Gustavo that his little obsession with coffee had reached beyond international borders.

"Listen, have you reviewed the e-mail I sent you last Friday?"

"No, not yet. I have over one hundred emails."

"Typical Monday morning," said the man from Dallas.

"Yeah," said Gustavo, "If you tell me the subject I'll look it up right now."

"Nah, it's a long post. Read it later, but ..." he paused. Gustavo understood he should focus his attention on the conversation. "It's about a boy named Miguel Delgado, who died three weeks ago. His parents are collecting on a million-dollar policy from us."

"Okay." Million-dollar policies were not uncommon any more.

"There's something weird with the documents they presented. The age on the birth certificate does not match the one on the death certificate."

"What's the difference?"

"Let me see." Gustavo heard the shuffling of papers at the other side of the line. "Four years."

Gustavo thought for a moment. "Until a few years ago, the registry would fine people who failed to declare a child's birth within thirty days. To avoid the fine, many parents used to lie about their kid's birthdate."

"Really? I didn't know that."

"That's why I have a job." Gustavo waited for Roger's chuckle to die down, then added, "I'll check the family's background."

"Yes, please. I want a full profile."

"Will do." He hung up after exchanging goodbyes and sat back on his chair and sipped from his treasured mug.

He calculated his commission if he discovered fraud: five percent of the saved amount totaled fifty thousand dollars. Bypassing the other emails, he searched for the Miguel Delgado dossier. The message included a copy of the signed policy, the payment request filed by the father, and about twenty pages of the prior reports with the company. It was too much to read on the computer screen so he printed the entire file.

Chapter Five

Puerto Barrios, Guatemala

Counting the hundred-dollar bills, Howard Gonzales exited the house. His nostrils filled with the unmistakable salty air typical of a port city. His five associates awaited him, gathered next to the minivan parked under the shade of a tall palm tree.

Howard opened the sliding door of the van and took up position there. The back of the front seat had a small table similar to those found on airplanes. He divided the money into four piles, as he had already separated Marcos's and his own share before coming out. He gave the even piles to his three mechanics and Carlos.

"I thought we'd lost that Hyundai," commented Manuel.

"Not a chance. I was certain Marcos would find a way." Howard saw Marcos's chest inflate with pride. "That car came with a very expensive price tag, though."

Marcos nodded as he raised his hand. At first, Howard thought Marcos was making a peace sign but then realized he had three fingers up. The number of kills.

Gregorio fidgeted. "Are we spending the night here?"

"Don't change the subject. Because of you, I had to kill the car owner, the passenger, and now that damn fat bastard." Marcos lowered his hand.

"It wasn't my fault!"

"Nevertheless, it happened. And no, we're not staying this time. After crossing the border, we'll go separate ways into San Pedro Sula," said Marcos. He and Howard had already made plans. "We meet back in Highland Creek in two weeks."

Howard noticed Carlos looking from Marcos to him, fidgeting. "Carlos," he barked and the young man went rigid. "Spill it."

"It's just that—"

"Come on, don't waste the colonel's time!" snapped Marcos.

Carlos took a deep breath, as if making up his mind, "Remember the last time we were pulled over and the cops looked like they were ready to bust us?"

"Of course, any cop would be nervous to find big six guys traveling together, you moron."

"I've thought of a way around that."

Howard detected a trace of pride – Carlos was trying to please him.

"You thought?" taunted Marcos, his right eyebrow arched high.

"Go on. What do you have in mind?" Howard stared at Marcos.

"Well ..." As if the prompt from Howard had bolstered his resolve, Carlos explained his idea. "Last month my wife and I went to a weekend retreat led by our pastor. To help pay for the expenses, the church sold T-shirts. I bought six of them and have them in my bag. I figured we could wear them and, if any cops stop us, they will think we are going to church."

Marcos burst into laughter and, as if on cue, the three mechanics joined in. Carlos's face flushed, as if he regretted what he had just said. Howard remained straight-faced. He admired Carlos's quiet inventiveness.

"Like wolves in sheep's clothing." The other four men fell silent. It was Marcos's turn to color. Howard decided it was rage rather than embarrassment. It was a shame Marcos was so shortsighted. Howard didn't like to put him down like this, even after what happened back at the border, but his second-in-command had asked for it. "I've always thought the Bible to be the greatest battle manual of all time."

"Does your pastor know where you get your income from?" Marcos said. Howard identified with him, a soldier after all, and incapable of backing down.

"Well, I ..." Carlos looked sheepish as Marcos's barb hit the target.

"Let's do this. Carlos, bring the shirts here. I hope they fit."

Carlos rushed to the back of the car. A minute later, he returned with salmon-colored T-shirts, and passed them out to the group. Marcos grimaced, but after catching a stern look from Howard, he put on the T-shirt. It was tight and the sleeves looked ready to rip under the strain of his bulging biceps.

Howard's slimmer but taut frame did not share Marcos's problems.

"Let's go."

Without further ceremony, they climbed into the van and left.

CHAPTER SIX

DALLAS, TEXAS

Roger Simmons tried without success to cover his increasing baldness with the few remaining brown strands. He frowned at his reflection in the bathroom mirror.

"Where did all my hair go?" he mused.

He worried more about the shine on his head than about his growing belly. He figured a bald, bespectacled accountant did not look the part of a Section Chief, even when handpicked by the Chairman of the Board at Real American Insurance.

Roger knew his reputation as a bean counter, but couldn't care less about it. Once on the job, the first thing he did was propose to move his department out of Hartford, insurance capital of the world, to Dallas, a good central location. He presented a report listing the benefits of the move. Since his realm included the international division as well, the budget for transportation alone projected savings in the order of seven figures and received the blessing of the Board of Directors.

It amused him how many people didn't even consider it fraud to take on the insurance company, thinking they were entitled to some money in return for the premiums they'd paid. Many unethical people – he thought 'felons' was too strong a word – would like to take advantage. Roger's job focused on verifying the submitted information and identifying scheming policyholders in order to stop those payments.

"Sir, Mrs. Meyer is on line three," his secretary's voice sounded through the speaker, and brought him back to the present.

Roger walked out of his private bathroom and took his place behind his large mahogany desk. Sitting down on the plush black leather chair, he picked up the handset.

"Thank you, Grace. I'll take it." He punched the buttons to connect the call.

"Morning, Mrs. Meyer. This is Roger Simmons. What can I do for you?"

"I was told you're holding my husband's check."

"That's not exactly true, ma'am. My department merely investigates—"

"I need that money! Frank left me a hill of bills to pay!"

Roger understood the widow's dilemma. Although he seldom contacted policyholders in person, this case had been special since the beginning. He knew the details by heart. Frank Meyer had traveled to Honduras the previous year, on an alleged business trip, then vanished. Meyer even left the bags in the beach resort where he was last seen.

"I'm truly sorry, but it takes seven years to declare a missing person legally dead." He knew that Mrs. Meyer was trying to collect the insurance, insisting that her husband was dead. Roger had been expecting this call; the week prior, he had recommended withholding the payment.

"I really need your help," she pleaded.

Roger suspected the husband had run away, maybe with a younger woman. The fact that Meyer had cleaned out his bank account before leaving served to endorse his theory. Still, he understood the woman's difficult situation.

"I'll look into it again. Would you mind if I send

somebody to ask a few questions?" He'd ask Gustavo Fonseca pay the hotel a visit and check things out.

"Not at all."

"Good. We'll be in touch, then."

"Thank you," she said between sobs.

Roger hung up the phone and sighed.

"Mr. Simmons, I have Mr. Sebastian Martin here to see you." Grace's voice came through the intercom.

Roger pressed the speaker button this time. "Tell him to come in, please."

Within seconds, a man stepped in. Roger rose from his chair and extended his hand in greeting. He noted how the man towered over him.

Sebastian walked the length of the office in two long strides and shook hands. Sebastian's rough and rather large hand swallowed Roger's in a firm grip. Roger valued firm handshakes and made a mental note as Sebastian introduced himself.

"Uncle Mike often speaks about you," said Sebastian.

Roger caught a lingering trace of alcohol in the man's breath but decided against making any comment about it. At least for the time being.

"We've been friends for twenty years. Did he ever tell you how we met?"

"Yes. He told the story every Thanksgiving dinner he shared with us." Sebastian's smile indicated more amusement than annoyance.

Roger smiled. "I bet my children heard the story just as often." He directed Sebastian to the seats. "Would you like something to drink?"

"The lady outside said she'd bring me a Coke."

Sebastian had just finished speaking when Grace walked in carrying a tray with two glasses filled with ice and bottled soft drinks.

"I brought you one as well, Mr. Simmons."

Roger thanked her as she placed the tray on his desk.

Sebastian nodded his thanks and she walked out of the office, careful to close the door behind her.

Roger reached for his drink, the diet cola, and poured his glass almost to the rim. He watched his guest do the same. "How was your trip down? I couldn't believe you drove all the way."

"Not a big fan of flying these days."

"I can imagine. Mike told me. Sorry about your loss."

Sebastian managed to shrug. Roger had done hundreds of job interviews but this was the first time he'd felt such awkwardness, almost as if he was the interviewee.

"Did Mike tell you what I'm looking for?" Roger thought it safe to steer the conversation to practical matters.

Sebastian nodded as he sipped from his glass. "He said it was about investigating insurance fraud."

"That's it in a nutshell, yes. You have no idea how many people like to present medical bills for treatments they didn't have, or stolen cars that are safely hidden in a friend's garage."

"Or people setting their own houses on fire," Sebastian put in.

"Right. There you go. Mike told me you investigated arson for the Fire Department in New York for the last few years."

"Now I see where my experience fits into this."

"Beg your pardon?" The comment puzzled Roger.

"It's just that I wasn't sure what a firefighter could do in an insurance company. Uncle Mike wasn't very specific."

Roger smiled. "What did you expect? He needs to leave some loopholes for negotiation. He's a lawyer after all."

Sebastian chuckled. "What is it that I can do for you, Mr. Simmons?"

The ball was back in his court and he had to make the

next move whether he liked it or not. They stared at each other for about a minute, neither willing to utter a word, resembling the gun duels of the old west. It felt like high noon to Roger. He knew about Sebastian's issues with boarding planes, and he understood them. But the fact was that the position on offer required him to move around a lot.

"I have an opening for an operative to investigate insurance fraud for the company. However, the job requires some traveling."

"Abroad?"

"Not often, but it might happen. I'll be honest with you. I see your fear of flying as a big drawback, regardless of being recommended by one of my best friends." He regretted being so tactless.

"I agree. The only reason I'm here is because Uncle Mike begged me to come."

Roger tried to maintain his composure but knew his face registered his anger. "Listen, Mr. Martin. I've conducted my share of job interviews and this is the first time I've seen someone so desperate *not* to be hired!"

"What!" Sebastian's lips formed a thin line parallel with his eyebrows as he frowned.

"I don't know how drunk you got last night and I don't care what your poison of choice was," Roger went on, "but I get a whiff of it every time you open your mouth. Now you dare to tell me that you wouldn't even be here if Mike hadn't begged you. What the hell are you playing at?"

Roger saw with satisfaction that his visitor closed his fist, the knuckles turning white before he spoke.

"You wouldn't understand. Do you know what it is to lose a son?" He spoke through clenched teeth.

"Yes, I do!" He was pleased to see this revelation caught Sebastian off guard.

It was true; he had lost a son. The baby died within

hours of being born. He knew the circumstances were different but the fact that he'd also lost a child served to disarm Sebastian.

"And let me tell you something else," continued Roger, "we have yet another thing in common. You are sitting there only because Mike asked me to see you."

"Then, let's stop wasting our time." Sebastian rose from his chair and left. He slammed the door behind him.

Roger sighed, angry and frustrated. He conjectured that this was perhaps the worst job interview he had ever conducted. I must be losing my touch with people, along with my hair. Gee, I'm also becoming cynical.

Chapter Seven

Near Dallas, Texas

The air conditioner in the metallic-green Chevy Blazer decided to fail at the same time Kenny Rogers sang the last notes of 'Lady' on the radio.

"Damn! Just my luck." Sebastian Martin fumbled with the controls and got nothing but hot air out of the vents.

He gave up with a sigh. He hit the switches on the door to lower the windows. A warm breeze disheveled his longer-than-usual light brown hair and refreshed him. He ran his right hand through the windswept mess, straightening and tidying it, as the breeze tangled it again in no time. Redirecting his thoughts, he pushed the auto dial button on the radio and found another country music station. Five more attempts and he was convinced that country was indeed the most popular music in Texas.

He focused on the road; the highway stretched without curves to the horizon. Traffic was scarce. He thought it was odd but he pushed the notion aside as a headache hammered inside his skull. He felt it sneak up on him the instant the air conditioner died.

Up ahead, a green sign with white letters announced he was five miles from the Golden Seven Ranch.

He pressed the accelerator, disabling the cruise control, for the last sprint. Then he turned left onto an unpaved detour. The pasture looked a deep shade of green, ready to turn brown for the changing season.

Trees were scarce but what trees there were had huge trunks and provided partial shade from the blinding sun over the grazing grounds on both sides of the wooden fence.

"Summer Bar-B-Q, yeah. Great!" he exclaimed.

Mike had told him it was a small ranch, but it didn't look small to him. As he neared the two-story white clapboard house, he noticed more cars than the driveway was intended hold. Among the parked cars, he recognized his uncle Michael's silver gray BMW.

He parked behind the last car and killed the engine. It felt good to stretch his legs after an hour behind the wheel.

He walked in between trucks of all shapes and sizes. Monster-sized double-axle trucks sat alongside more modest Ford 150s. All had the power to move what ranchers needed moved most – livestock. Or maybe they were some yuppie macho display. He'd seen that often enough. Trucks littered the highway, hogged fuel, roared and grandstanded, with not so much as a nick, or scratch or a heavy-duty mark to indicate they'd ever been used for more than tossing a bag of groceries in the back. Not the proud duty for which the massive machines were intended, that's for sure.

At the front door, he knocked. A distant female voice called out, "Coming." When the door opened, a woman in her mid-thirties dressed in blue jeans and a white polo shirt stood in the entrance.

"You must be Sebastian," she said.

"How—"

"You're the only one missing. My father and Mike have been talking about you," she explained.

"Nothing bad I hope." He hid his irritation at being a casual topic of conversation behind a smile.

"Don't worry about it." Her smile looked sincere.

Sebastian returned the smile. He worried she might

have inherited her father's sense of smell and detect the liquor he'd consumed the night before. A second later, he felt silly for fretting about such things.

"I'm Jill Simmons. Please come in." She tossed back her long dark brown hair as she held the door for him.

Once inside, he followed her to the other side of the house. A sliding glass door led out to the terrace and the vast expanse of the ranch beyond.

He whistled, impressed. "I was told this was a small place, but it looks big enough."

"Thank you, but it is small by comparison. It's sad the whole family can't come as often as I'd like. But I'm enjoying it a lot these days." The smile was gone; she looked saddened somehow, as if someone had passed over her grave. Sebastian decided not to ask.

She opened the sliding door and led him to the right. Four tables were set out on the wooden deck; each rested under the shadow of a huge umbrella.

Roger Simmons walked over to meet them. He was clad in a red, green, and white plaid shirt, faded black jeans, and black leather boots. A black cowboy hat covered his bald head.

Where're the spurs? Sebastian thought with a smirk. "Nice hat," he said instead, as he shook hands with Roger.

"Thank you. It's a Stetson original. It cost more than the tires on that Chevy you rented." He said it with a straight face and a fake heavy drawl.

"Sorry I'm late, got lost." The shame that he had overslept, after consuming three quarters of bottle of vodka the evening before, suppressed the slight wave of remorse about lying.

"Happens a lot, don't worry. I was afraid you weren't coming after our short-lived meeting yesterday."

"About that, Mr. Simmons—"

"Please, call me Roger," he cut him off. "It's all right.

35

I said some things out of turn myself. Let's put that behind us. Come meet the family." His stoic expression dissolved into a smile.

Roger led Sebastian to the first table and introduced him to an older version of the woman who opened the door, except she was blonde.

"This is my wife, Mary," he began. "You met Jill at the door. On her right is Sandy and on Mary's left is Roger Jr."

"Dad! Stop calling me junior." The young man seemed annoyed.

"Stop complaining. You're the favorite anyway," commented Sandy with a twisted scowl, revealing sibling rivalry, her words edged with a hint of anger.

Sebastian thought of James. Ah, been there, done that. He knew Sandy Simmons worked at Uncle Mike's law firm. She looked the part of a competent lawyer: short blonde hair, rather elegant. She was dressed in a blue blouse that favored her inquisitive eyes and linen skirt. Sebastian guessed she would not be riding horses today.

Sebastian had the impression of a happy and loving family. His mind drifted back to his dead wife and boy, and how happy they would have been. He came back to reality when he felt a heavy slap on the back.

"Was afraid you weren't coming,"

"Hi, Uncle Mike. Your car out there stands out like a sore thumb among so many trucks." Sebastian put out his hand.

"You noticed that, huh?" His hair combed back, perfect as usual, thought Sebastian.

"Yeah, I did." He leaned forward so the rest of the group wouldn't hear him. "And what's with the cowboy theme? I know they love that stuff here, but I see horns on cars, and the radio won't play anything but country music. I mean, come on, do you ever get used to that?"

"Welcome to Texas, son!"

Roger introduced him to the other guests.

"We get this Bar-B-Q instead of a well-deserved bonus," joked the last woman who shook his hand.

"Thank you, Grace, I'll sure remember that in December," countered Roger, the drawl gone.

Sebastian went back to the first table and took a seat next to Michael. "Where's Brenda?" he asked.

"She's visiting her parents in Los Angeles," he explained.

Sebastian felt the best definition for Brenda Smith was 'trophy wife.' She was tall, blonde, blue eyed, big breasted, and sported a tiny waist that at the age of thirty could only be maintained with a surgeon's skill. Michael had married her two years before because it was advisable for a lawyer to have a wife and family; he said it gave the impression to his clients that lawyers were human after all. Sebastian and James had laughed about it over dinner one night. James's wife, Christine, and Kelly had scolded them for it.

"Is her sister coming to visit again?" asked the younger Roger who sat across the table.

"I don't know, but she's only seventeen. Too young for you!" joked Michael.

"She won't be by the time I finish med school. I'm just sowing the seed," explained the young man with a wink.

"Men are all alike," complained Jill.

An awkward silence enveloped the table. Sebastian turned to see Jill fighting to contain tears. She rose and ran inside the house.

"She's been through a nasty divorce. She found her husband cheating with an eighteen-year-old girl," explained Michael in a very low voice.

"She's passing time here at the ranch," added Sandy.

"She's a CPA like Dad, so she's got a job she can bring home to fill her time," finished Roger Jr.

Every family has skeletons in their closets, Sebastian concluded. On the surface, Roger Simmons had it all: a good influential position in one of the largest insurance companies in the country, a beautiful wife and kids, good life-long friends like Michael Smith. It wasn't Jill's fault her husband had cheated on her, but how good they all came together for her. Much like James was looking after him now, he reflected.

CHAPTER EIGHT

NEAR DALLAS, TEXAS

Roger Simmons saw his daughter running from the table. He traded a knowing look with Mary and she went after their second born. A small consolation to him was that he had helped her find a job that she could do from the ranch. The time away from the city had done her some good.

All morning she had looked happy, joking around with her brother and sister. His father's instinct told him it must have been a comment that brought back memories of that bastard. He had hated his son-in-law from the moment he'd met him and attended the wedding only out of respect for his daughter. It was one of the few times he regretted being proved right.

After Jill left the table, Roger watched Mike, Sandy, and Roger Jr. speaking in hushed tones. He figured that by now Sebastian Martin was fully briefed on Jill's problems. He felt a bit embarrassed it had happened in front of the guests, but more important, in front of a stranger and potential employee like Mr. Martin.

After the sour-ending interview with Sebastian Martin, Roger had called Michael to complain.

"What kind of guy did you send me here, Mike? He doesn't want to work!"

"I know, but he has to, or he'll go nuts."

"If you ask me, he's there already. Driving all the way from New York to interview for a job he doesn't want."

"I said it might be a long shot."

"You also said it was worth it."

"And you think it isn't?" Mike had sounded upset.

"To tell you the truth, I am not impressed at all."

"Oh, really? Contact his boss at the Fire Department. If you don't change your opinion after you've checked him out, I'll never bother you again. Do we have a deal?"

Roger had considered the proposal for a minute; at the same time, he cooled down.

"Roger, are you still there?" The silence must have made Mike wonder.

"Do you ever get to go to court? You seem very good at cutting deals," Roger had said with a smile.

He'd followed the counselor's advice and called friends in New York to make discreet inquiries about Sebastian Martin. The report he received changed his opinion of the man.

Not only was Sebastian a distinguished member of New York's Bravest, but for the past five years had worked investigating arson. Something he did so well, he'd lectured all over the country – even once in France. He figured that trip was before Sebastian developed an aversion for airplanes.

What impressed Roger the most was that the Chief of Section took the time to call Roger, asking him to give Lieutenant Martin a chance. He told Roger they knew that after the accident Sebastian was not up for walking into flaming buildings anymore, no matter how much therapy he received.

At five o'clock Roger had called Mike to invite Sebastian to the Bar-B-Q to try to get to know him better.

Given a second chance, Sebastian Martin saw fit to arrive late and attempt to get away with using a lame excuse. The smell of liquor gave the lie to that bullshit story of getting lost.

Roger understood the reasons behind Martin's self-destructive behavior; it was survivor's guilt. The poor widower felt it unfair to be alive when his wife and boy died beside him. Roger had seen it all before.

A whiff of burnt meat brought him back to the task in hand.

After lunch, Roger asked who would like to go horseback riding. Most of the guests declined but Mike and Sebastian were up for it. As the three men walked toward the stable, Roger decided to cut the guy some slack.

"How do you like Texas so far?" he asked.

Sebastian shrugged. "It's nice. Don't get me wrong but a true New Yorker will never feel comfortable any place other than in the Big Apple."

"Mike has lived here almost twenty years," Roger said, jerking a thumb at the lawyer who walked next to him.

Mike was prompt in defending his case. "That's different. I was running away from my family."

"Why did you name the ranch Golden Seven?" Sebastian asked, changing the subject and making Roger wonder why.

"Oh, that's a long family story. I'll tell you the short version. I was premature so I was nicknamed Golden Seven. You know, born at seven instead of nine months. It didn't stick but I kind of liked it. Mary knew the story, of course. It was her idea," said Roger. "It gives the place a nice touch."

Roger pointed at the open stable door. "Well, here we are." A man came out with five saddled horses. "This is Jack Taylor. He takes care of the ranch for me," Roger explained.

"Howdy." Jack stretched out his hand.

"Sebastian Martin."

Jack traded a look with Mike, then with Roger and back to Sebastian. "Is this the guy who was named after Sebastian Walbo, the poet?"

"Yep," Sebastian admitted at the same time as he elbowed his uncle in the ribs.

Roger suppressed a smile. Mike really was a blabbermouth when it came to the people he cared for. Mike had told them how Sebastian hated his name and being asked about the famous poet so often. Oh, if the firefighter only knew he was in for a surprise.

"Yeah, well. What do you think of my Quarter Horses?" asked Roger. "So called because they can outdistance other breeds in races of a quarter mile, or less."

"They're imposing. How tall are they – six feet?"

Roger couldn't contain his smile this time.

Jack Taylor did not even try. "No damned self-respecting cowboy would measure a horse in feet, boy," exclaimed Taylor with his heavy Texan drawl.

"We measure height at the withers," said Roger, caressing the ridge between the shoulder blades on the closest animal to illustrate, "and we use hands. A hand is about four inches, right, Jack?"

"You got that right, boss."

"Oh, that explains the laughter," said Sebastian. "Do they at least have names?"

"Yep," said Jack, and pointed at each horse as he said its name with affection. "Rambo, Mango, Walbo, Tango, and Cash."

"Cash?"

"Ran out of rhymes," explained Jack shrugging.

"And you like poetry, too? Naming one of them after a poet, I mean."

"Oh, no, not me. This gelding was born an ugly duckling. It was on its way to the butcher when Jill vouched for it. She named it Walbo," explained Roger, remembering happier times before Jill got married.

"I asked Jack to saddle that horse in the middle for you, Seb," said Mike. He had been altogether too quiet for a lawyer, and had a sly smile lighting up his face.

"Bet you did." Without another word, Sebastian took the reins of a different one.

"That would be Cash," interjected Roger.

After they mounted, Roger led them on an easy trot around the ranch. Roger always felt happy on his range. Of course, he didn't have the time or the stamina to care for it the way he wanted to. When he bought the ranch, at Mary's insistence, he hired Jack Taylor, who came with his Mexican wife, Gabriela. Their only offspring, Jack Jr., became best friend to his own son. Nice pair they made: Roger blond and Jack dark, after their respective mothers. They were always playing in the nearby town, pretending to be the characters in the Dukes of Hazard. They were only missing a couple of Daisies, they always claimed. Jack Jr. was now off to college to study journalism on a full scholarship.

"How big is this ranch?" asked Sebastian, bringing Roger out of his reverie.

"Oh, twelve acres, overall. State law mandates that I have at least an acre per horse, so I don't over populate. As you saw I have only five geldings so I'm all right, with room to spare."

"Gelding. I heard that word back there. What does it mean?"

"It means a horse has been castrated," he explained.

Roger smiled when he saw the typical reaction of men. Sebastian cringed as he attempted to bring his legs as close together as the mount would allow.

Roger found Sebastian an easy man to talk to; the firefighter seemed relaxed and not pushed against a wall, as he had at the office. Perhaps he had been a bit too rough with him on their first encounter. They passed the afternoon away trotting around on horses.

As the sun moved on its way toward twilight, out of the corner of his eye, he saw someone approaching. He turned to see Jill coming from the stable riding Walbo.

"I just told Sebastian the story of your mount," he yelled to his daughter.

"Dad! Can't you let it go?" she called back, in good humor.

Good, thought Roger with relief, the crisis must be over.

Jill was about ten feet away when Walbo reared, neighing and snorting in fear. The horse brought down its front legs on the earth, only to rear up again, terrified.

Roger watched in shock as Jill flew off the back of the saddle and fell on the ground with a heavy thud. She screamed in pain. She screamed again, her hands clutching her leg.

Roger found himself rooted to his saddle, unable to comprehend what was happening. He opened his mouth, trying to say something, as he saw the origin of the commotion – a long narrow snake with light-colored reddish-brown marks.

To his horror, he realized that Jill had fallen almost on top of it and the snake, instinctively, had bitten her on the closest spot, her ankle.

Sebastian dismounted and rushed toward her. Walbo reared once more. This time the animal found its mark and brought its heavy horseshoes on top of the snake's head, crushing it.

Roger also dismounted, his heart drumming on his chest. Every step toward Jill felt eternal, like walking underwater. He opened and closed his fists in desperation.

He approached Sebastian from behind. "Be careful," he warned, "snakes are known to bite even after they're dead. It's a reflex." Feeling helpless as a spectator, he paced quickly behind Sebastian.

Roger watched as Sebastian ripped the leg of Jill's pant, exposing the twin, small round bite marks. A thin thread of red blood ran down to her foot.

Sebastian looked around as if trying to find something. "I need a knife! I'm assuming the snake is poisonous!"

"What?"

"A switchblade, a knife – anything with an edge! Come on; don't tell me all you have are Winchesters!"

Roger never carried a weapon, but automatically patted himself down. Only to confirm what he already knew: that it was a futile effort. Statistical reports of snakebites had come across his desk. Some snakebites were deadly if not treated right away. The idea of Jill becoming a number in those reports appalled him. "Not my little girl, God. Please." His prayer did little to calm him.

"Damn it," Sebastian said. He pulled out his car key and looked at it.

"Wait!" Mike fished out a small Swiss Army knife from his pocket. The kind used as key rings. "Would this one work?" Mike passed it to Sebastian.

The fireman ripped the fabric further up Jill's leg, ignoring her scream of pain. Sebastian pulled the blade out and cut the ripped denim into strips. He tied the longest strip around her leg, a tourniquet, about an inch below the knee, to prevent the poison from traveling upward.

"She needs medical assistance," he called over his shoulder before he applied his mouth to the bite and sucked, then spat. He repeated the process a couple of times.

"I thought sucking from the wound of a snakebite was outdated."

"It works best if done soon enough. Besides, I'm old-school. Get her an ambulance."

Roger turned to face Mike, "The nearest hospital is fifty minutes away in either direction!" Now he regretted buying the ranch, and having Quarter horses. He despised himself for planning the Bar-B-Q, but above all, he now considered the idea of going out on a ride this afternoon as ridiculous and stupid.

Mike pulled out his cell phone and dialed. "Hi, this is an emergency. A snake bit a woman ... We're at the Golden Seven Ranch on the Interstate." He paused to listen to a question from the operator. "No, I don't know what type of snake!" he screamed as he shook his head.

"A copperhead!" Roger shouted.

"What?" Mike put a hand over the phone's speaker.

"Tell them it was a copperhead and that we have it," said Roger, not taking his eyes off his daughter.

"Okay." He returned to his call, "it's a copperhead, and we have it. It's dead. No, damn it, I didn't kill it! The horse stomped on it. Yes, a horse! No, we need a chopper." Mike walked off with the phone pressed hard against his ear.

Roger turned his head and saw his friend's back as he walked a few paces. He could not hear the conversation anymore. That was so typical of Mike, he reflected, walking around when talking on the phone.

Distraught, he turned his attention back to his daughter. Roger knelt next to Sebastian and watched as he finished tying the tourniquet. Jill was still conscious and sweating profusely.

"Daddy," she moaned.

He felt his heart shrivel with anguish. He had let her down. In complete impotence, he envisioned his daughter dying. It was his fault. All his fault! Damn snakes, damn horses. I'm an accountant, and should stick to what I'm good at – numbers! Roger caressed her face as he bit his lower lip, holding back a tear. "What can I do?" he pleaded as he looked at Sebastian.

"Nothing here." He made the knot tighter.

"Aaahh ..." The cry escaped before Jill could bite her

lip to suppress it.

"Easy there." Roger patted her shoulder.

"I know what I'm doing." Sebastian tied a second knot.

Roger glared at Sebastian, who ignored him and continued his work. Roger's anger subsided as he watched Sebastian's efficiency, the steady pulse, the way he had taken command. All contributed to Roger's new appraisal of Sebastian. He recalled the phone call from New York. Now he understood what the others saw in the man who now tended to his daughter. He looked around. Mike had ended the phone call and was walking back toward them. He stopped a moment to grab Walbo's reins. The horse neighed, but stayed put when Mike caressed its large head.

"Dad ..."

Large drops of perspiration formed on Jill's forehead. Roger prayed they were because of the heat and not the fever. When he swiped the sweat away, her skin felt hot.

"She's feverish."

"That's a good sign. It means her system is fighting," Sebastian said.

Mike stepped up behind them. "A chopper is coming in under ten minutes. The damned operator didn't want to send it until I gave her my credit card number!"

"Jill has full insurance." At least he could be proud of that. He had made sure his family had the best insurance cover money could buy.

"I know, Roger. Don't worry, I think it was more to prove it wasn't a prank call."

Roger exhaled with some relief. A snakebite was not unheard of in Texas, even if it was the first time it had happened to any member of his family. He knew with immediate care, the patient had a better chance of survival. But ten minutes? That wasn't immediate – that was an eternity.

Chapter Nine

Dallas, Texas

Sebastian sat on a couch in the hospital waiting area with the rest of Jill's family. After the helicopter took off with Jill and her father, he and Uncle Mike returned to the house and informed the family. He drove back to his hotel to drop off his car and then rode with Uncle Mike to the hospital.

The faces of the people around showed their worries and fears and resurrected his own. The last time he'd been in a hospital, James had sat by his side, and placed a hand on his shoulder when the police officers confirmed his wife and son were dead. Just the memory made his breathing falter as the pressure in his chest escalated. He couldn't stand it. He needed a drink. To avoid the urge, he pretended to read a magazine he found on the coffee table, dated from the previous year.

A doctor dressed in the usual green scrubs walked out of a set of double doors. Jill's parents flew from the sofa with anxious expressions. Sebastian rose and approached the worried couple.

"She was brought here in good time and since we were certain on the type of snake, the right antidote has been administered. It will be a painful recovery, but she'll be fine," the doctor concluded. "If everything is okay, she'll be released by noon tomorrow."

"Can we see her?" asked Jill's mother.

The doctor nodded. "She's asleep. You can go in a

moment, but first I must warn you, the swelling is normal. This is one of the cases where things look worse than they are."

Sebastian was touched to see Roger breathe a sigh of relief and watched as Mary embraced her husband with tears of joy on her face. After a second, Mary let him go, and turned to face Sebastian.

"I can't thank you enough," she said.

He tried to explain he hadn't done anything special, but Mary was already putting her arms around him. He returned the embrace. Standing back, she graced his cheek with a kiss. She was a grateful mother, and a good woman. Roger Jr. and Sandy came to embrace him, too.

Uncle Mike returned with a cup in his hand. Roger embraced him with such force that the coffee slurped out and burnt Mike's hand.

"*Ouch.*" Uncle Mike put the cup on the table and blew in his hand. "Damn, it's hot."

"She's going to be okay." Roger said.

Mike's lips parted into a huge smile, as if he had just won his first court case. Free from the burn hazard, he embraced Roger and Mary.

Uncle Mike was right: these were good people. Roger's employees respected and admired him; he had observed that during the Bar-B-Q. Since arriving at the hospital, Roger's phone had rung without cease. So many people wanted to enquire about Jill.

Sebastian had seen such a brotherhood before, a million years ago, or so it seemed, at the Fire Station. There he had experienced the same feeling of belonging he had seen here. Firemen were just as close. It was the only way to put your life in someone else's hands; you had to trust the team. Otherwise, you were as good as dead.

He made a decision. A decision he had put off for too long.

"Roger, can I talk to you for a second?"

He nodded and together they moved a couple of paces out of earshot from the rest of his family.

"If the offer to work for you is still standing, I'll take it."

For a reply, Roger extended his hand. Sebastian shook it and saw a satisfied smile forming on the face of his new boss.

It was another job. Hell, it was another city.

He had found a group of people he thought he could work with.

It was time to resume his life.

CHAPTER TEN

The man leaned over the edge to peer inside the crater of the Masaya Volcano in Nicaragua. Dormant for over a hundred years, a constant plume of smoke rose from the depths of the pit. The heavy smell of sulfur made people sick and warnings not to stay more than twenty minutes were scattered along the site. Visitors could hike along the steep hillside on paths and even explore some natural and lava-made caverns.

"Don't do that!" the woman screeched.

"What?"

"It's dangerous."

"You think a tongue of flame will leap up to burn my face?" A trace of cynicism tinged his voice.

"No. I think a loose rock could cause you to slip and fall over the edge."

"Ah, okay then, there is that." He had not anticipated that reply.

"Really, stop joking around."

"Will you love me forever if I fall?" He extended his arms at shoulder length, resembling the crucified savior, and tilted dangerously toward the drop.

"No." Her face was very serious. "Maybe I'll mourn you for a year and then go after a rich husband."

"Oh, come on."

"I don't like it when you turn into this ... this childish guy."

"All right, all right." He lowered his hands and moved away from the edge. He pulled out a quarter from his pants pocket, took a moment to inspect the coin, as if searching for a flaw. He positioned it on top of his index and thumb, and flicked it.

The coin flipped through the air. At its highest point, it hung mid-air for a slow second, traversed the last part of the arc, and dropped into the mouth of the volcano.

"I've heard of people doing that at fountains, never lava pits," she said.

The man shrugged.

The coin continued whirling its way downward, until it came to rest atop a blackened rock. With no connection whatsoever to the dropped piece of metal, a slight tremor began.

The rumble gained momentum until the coin moved with violence. Then the tremor subsided as fast as it had begun. After a moment of silence, it turned out that the tremor was the preamble.

The eruption took the tourists by surprise. Hysterical screams filled the air as people ran down the path, screams of terror lost in the noise from the mountain. A crack appeared in the rock. The coin fell through the crevice only to be expelled a second later, engulfed by flames as it flew through the air.

Black smoke formed a mushroom cloud seen from miles away. In the nearby town, people rushed out in panic, looking for safety, fearing for their lives.

A six-year-old boy had trouble keeping up with his mother in the crowded streets. In her frenzy, she almost pulled the boy's arm out of its socket, half dragging him beside her. He looked back at the erupting volcano. Something glittering in the middle of his line of vision caught his attention. The object covered the distance, and came straight at the boy. Transfixed, he watched as if in slow motion. The shiny object hit him on the back of his right hand. At first, he felt nothing, then the assault on his senses, which began with a soft tingle, grew into a dreadful stinging. The smell of burnt flesh filled his nostrils. The pain peaked and he woke up, agitated and covered in sweat.

It was not the first time Howard Gonzales had had that particular dream. With his left hand, he touched the back of his other one. There it was, clearly visible, the eagle that graced one side of the U.S. quarter. He caught his breath, willing it back to normal while looking at the mark.

The truth was that he didn't remember how or why he'd been branded with the back of the quarter. He'd had it as long as he could remember and these dreams, he assumed, were his subconscious attempts to explain its presence.

Recruited by the Nicaraguan national army as a young boy, he became an easy target for his soldier mates. The teasing subsided after he'd broken the second arm and the third nose. He earned the necessary respect, and fear, to become a leader noticed by the KGB scouts.

He stretched to wake up, looked at his watch: 5:07a.m. He was late. His cell phone lit up but made no sound. He took the call.

"Sir, we've got one."

"Are you sure?"

"Yes, we deploy in twenty minutes."

Now awake, Howard smiled. It had been a slow month but if Marcos was correct, they were back in business.

Chapter Eleven

Dallas, Texas

Sebastian had not felt butterflies in his stomach in a long time. He woke early, bathed and shaved, took some time to choose his outfit and then ate a power bar on the way to work. At half past eight, he walked into the building but security would not let him enter. The guard informed him that he needed authorization.

At a quarter to nine, Grace arrived, vouched for him at the entrance and together they rode the elevator to the office.

"You won't have this problem tomorrow," she promised, "you'll be given a pass today."

"Thank you."

"You're welcome." The elevator doors slid open. "Follow me."

Sebastian followed her through the carpeted corridor. She walked with the passion of a person trying to beat the clock. They reached an office furnished with a pair of partners' desks facing each other.

"This is you. Take the desk on the left. Bill should arrive soon."

"Bill?"

"Oh, right. You haven't met him because he was out of town and missed the barbeque. William Knox is our senior investigator. He'll be your supervisor."

"Okay." He tried for a casual tone.

"Don't worry. Bill is one hell of a guy to work with.

He looks tough because his job demands it, but inside he is an old softy."

"If you say so."

Grace walked out leaving Sebastian in his new office. He walked to his recently assigned desk, the swivel chair, well padded and comfy, without a high back like the plush executive types. A desktop computer rested on top of the otherwise empty surface. Sebastian pushed the "on" button and was rewarded with an instant whine and hum. A welcome message flashed on the screen, then a prompt for a username and password.

"Figures! There goes my chance to play solitaire while I wait for this Bill guy to show up," he mused.

"That would be me." The voice came from the doorway. Sebastian stood to greet him. The man gave him a firm handshake.

Bill Knox looked to be in his late fifties. Ash blond hair kept a bit too long; almost as tall as Sebastian but not as wide; broad shoulders, but a small belly protruded under the loose polo shirt that he wore with the collar up. He took off the navy blue sport coat and hung it on the back of the chair. He fell into the chair with a weighty thump and crossed his legs. The ripped jeans ended on what Sebastian took to be snake leather boots. The most distinctive feature was the pair of steel blue eyes; the crooked nose only added to the tough guy look.

"You're that firefighter guy from New York, I reckon." The heavy Texan drawl made it unnecessary to ask about his origins.

Sebastian nodded.

"Welcome aboard, pal. Have a seat. We're gonna be here for a while."

Sebastian returned to his seat and eyed the computer. It had gone into screensaver mode and the company logo floated about the black background.

"Are we going to use this often?"

"Yep. Most reports you type in and send them by e-mail. The environmental freaks are taking over. The other day I received a mail with a legend that read, 'Do you really need to print this email?'" He chuckled.

"I've seen that one, too!"

"But no computer work today. Roger told me I have to train you."

"Train me?"

"Okay. Don't get all sensitive on me." He raised his hands in mock defense. "Show you the ropes sound better to you?"

It was Sebastian's turn to chuckle. "Yeah, ego intact."

The following hours passed in avid conversation. Despite the sometimes annoying drawl, every sentence that came out of Bill's mouth was a real milestone into Sebastian's journey through the world of insurance fraud. The man had seen it all. It surprised Sebastian to the point he felt overwhelmed. He learned that insurance was the business of selling a percentage that you play, not unlike placing a bet in a casino. You charge an amount – the premium – based on statistics. Bill explained the little-known intricacies of the business and illustrated with real cases: statistics showed smokers were more prone to develop cancer; ergo, smokers paid a higher premium.

"Follow the money trail. That's the key! For once, those Hollywood punks got it right. Best piece of advice I'll toss your way. For example," he pulled a file off the stack that had accumulated during their conversation, "this guy claims a thief broke in and stole the TV set, stereo, MP3 player and the list goes on and on. But when we requested the proofs of purchase, he had *nada*, zip."

"Not everybody saves the receipts."

"Okay, I'll give you that." He sat back, crossed his leg again. "Tell me this. How can I know for sure they robbed him of a plasma TV worth ten grand instead of a four hundred dollar big-ass Sharp?"

Sebastian took some time to think about that one. Bill was right. Without any proof of purchase, you could put anything on the claim. Long gone were the days when your word of honor was enough.

He looked back at Bill who sat back smiling with satisfaction. "You see it now."

"Never thought of it before."

"Most people never do. But, hey, I never thought to check the batteries twice a year on the smoke detector until a fireman inspecting the building told me. You ain't thought about it, because you ain't got no need to."

Sebastian figured the comment about his background as fireman was intended to make him see that he was not stupid, just had stuff to learn about a new business. Grace had been right about Bill as a good mentor.

"In short, you are like a detective."

"No, but I do detective work. I go out and see the things myself. Then make a report and recommendation on whether to pay or not."

"Do you travel a lot?"

"I move around Texas and states close by. Farther out we keep locals on retainers or pay them a percentage of the policy. But some cases I have to oversee."

"You trust these guys?"

"Sure, after a couple of years. Some I supervise more than others, of course."

Opening another folder, Bill pulled out a single sheet of paper and handed it to Sebastian. "Pop quiz. Read that and tell me what you think."

"Okay." Sebastian scanned the sheet and looked up again after a minute. "Is he for real?"

"Afraid so." Bill shrugged. "Now tell me what you think."

After a sigh, Sebastian chose his words with great care.

"The submission sheet has no blanks left. Every 't' is crossed as my English teacher wanted. The fact that he's near-sighted since he was a teenager makes it a pre-existing condition, thus not subject to the policy. I cannot see the connection between a car accident – even if he broke the windshield with his face – and an operation to correct his vision." Sebastian looked at a nodding Bill and, reassured, he summed it up. "I think the insurance policy holder is trying to recoup what he paid for his premium."

"And then some. Nice to see you got the lingo down right."

The following day Sebastian found Bill already sitting at his desk. As he walked in, Bill announced, "We're having a field trip today."

With the skill of a New York taxi driver, Bill steered them out of the city. "I hate those damn GPS pieces of crap. Give me a map and I'll get there!" Despite the driving, Sebastian counted his blessings: Bill's aircon worked.

They rode for well over an hour beyond the city limits, in a different direction from Roger's ranch. Still, the scenery was pretty much the same. Tall buildings shrank as they left them behind. In their place, Sebastian saw large tracts of land without as much as a house. After a while, they took a secondary road. Sebastian read the name of the property on an old, weather-beaten sign, THE HEAVENSENT EGG FARM.

"What are we doing here?"

"We came to assess the damage. The ranch owners reported almost a million bucks in losses. As per the report, the air conditioner failed and a whole bunch of chickens died."

"Interesting."

"Now, we are not here to judge 'em or their facilities even if you think they're crap. I don't want you to comment on whatever you see. Just observe and then tell me back in the car. Is that clear?"

"Yes. But why? I thought our job was to judge the claim."

"For one thing, you owe them some respect. So you show 'em that. Also, you want to avoid confrontation. Your opinion might not be appreciated. Heck, some folk could hate you right then and there!"

"I get it."

"Do you? Really?"

"Yes, I do." Sebastian repeated with every ounce of conviction he could muster.

After they exited from the main road, they followed an unpaved driveway up to the main building, which was nothing more than an oversized trailer. Bill pulled up and parked next to two trucks already parked outside. They got out and walked to the door.

Looking at the other two large buildings on the opposite side, Sebastian could not ignore the sense of despair hanging in the air.

Bill let himself in without even knocking. Sebastian heard a soft hum and appreciated the much cooler interior.

"Hi, there," called a man clad in brown boots, blue jeans, a plaid shirt and the obligatory cowboy hat.

Bill smiled. "Hi. We're from the insurance company."

"Oh, yes. They called and said you were coming." The man approached and extended his hand, "I'm Charlie Boyd."

Charlie shook hands with both men. Bill wasn't one to waste time on pleasantries, so after introducing himself and Sebastian, he got down to business. Charlie led them through the farm in what seemed to Sebastian a record time.

There were four more barn-like buildings for the poultry. They all had the same decrepit timeworn look about them. Three of the buildings were occupied. Entering them was an assault on the senses. The smell of thousands of birds held together in confined space, and the taste of loose feathers, stuck in Sebastian's throat when he spoke. And the noise! Clucking filled the air.

Charlie answered all their questions. "During the summer days, we use the aircon system, if not, the animals would suffocate. They're so delicate we drive 'em to the slaughterhouse at night or else they don't make it alive."

They followed Charlie to the last building; it was as silent as midnight in a graveyard. Sebastian felt the air polluted with the ghosts of the dead birds.

"When I came in the morning to shovel the droppings, I found them all dead."

The extent of the job details felt unnecessary to Sebastian. He was fine not thinking or acknowledging his chicken legs were living creatures with all of the natural functions. He forced the thought out of his mind. Instead, he concentrated on the sweat that had accumulated on his forehead. He wiped it clean with his hand while he estimated the temperature inside the building to be somewhere in the high nineties.

"And then?" Bill's question brought him out of his reverie.

"The stench was awful, and the heat was worse than it is now. I called the boss and he brought a technician."

"A vet?"

"We needed no damn vet to tell us them chickens were dead! An electrical technician. He fixed the air conditioner."

"Did he?" It didn't feel like it, thought Sebastian, as he watched Bill wipe the sweat from his forehead with the back of his hand.

"Well, we won't turn it on until the new batch gets here."

"Makes sense, but we still need to see the unit working. Can you show us the control panels?"

"Sure." Charlie walked to the left corner of the building.

The wall was bare except for two large Square D electrical panels screwed in side by side. Charlie opened the one on the left.

"The unit is turned on from here. The system is automatic and runs on a thermostat dial fixed atop the panel." He hit two switches and the air filled with a soft hum.

"It takes a while to cool this large space. That's why we power them up a couple of hours before the truck arrives."

Sebastian opened the right hand panel and his fire-department trained eye inspected each of the switches, lined up in two columns. The last one down on the left caught his attention. The otherwise standard gray metal was black around the switch.

He ran a finger gently over it and something stuck to his skin instantly. He brought his finger close to his nose. The smell was familiar; it belonged to burned out cables and fuses not carefully replaced. A sloppy electrical job had created a fire hazard.

Sebastian traded looks with Bill. His boss raised an eyebrow to remind him of his terse warning back in the car. Sebastian nodded. Charlie took no notice of the exchange and he shut the panel down before leading visitors out.

Chapter Twelve

San Pedro Sula, Honduras

Living the bachelor life in San Pedro Sula after his divorce, Gustavo Fonseca was content with an apartment his few possessions could fill. He leased a small place from a widow who had converted her grand old house into three apartments. Each one had a kitchenette, a living room, and a bedroom. The widow lived in one, alone, her kids all grown and gone. She lived on the rent from the other two.

Gustavo arrived with a companion for the night. Rosa Murillo held the white paper bag with the Subway sandwiches they bought on the way. They walked between the secondhand sofa his mother had given him and the counter that divided the kitchenette space from the lounge. He dropped a folder on the countertop, looked at the answering machine blinking the loneliest of numbers. One message. Rosa settled on the couch while he pressed the button and walked to the fridge.

The machine announced the date and time of the message, then, "Hi, Dad!" The shrieking voice of his fourteen-year-old son filled the room. "I lost my cellphone along with your cell number. Can you call me at home?"

Gustavo grabbed two Cokes out of the fridge, took one can to Rosa, and left the other one on the counter top. On top of ice in a tall glass, he poured a generous measure of golden rum, then topped it with the cola and used his index finger to stir the mix.

Rosa watched him. "Can we eat now?"

"You go ahead, precious. I have to return this call." Gustavo took the handset and dialed.

"Hi, Susana. How are you?" He was past all the bitterness with his ex-wife.

"I'm good. I interviewed my first case study today." She had gone back to school and was a year shy of her psychology degree.

"Hey, that sounds great!"

"Isn't it?" She bubbled with excitement.

"Yep. I knew you'd make it. Listen, could you pass me to Gustavo? He called me earlier."

"Of course." She hesitated a bit before adding, "Did you make it to the bank today?"

"Yes, I transferred the alimony this afternoon. It should appear on your account by tomorrow."

"Oh, that's great. Gustavo needs new jeans. That boy is growing too fast. Hold on, here he is."

"Hi, Dad. Was she nagging you about money again?"

"Just a mother-bear looking after her cubs. That's all."

"Whatever."

Gustavo pictured his son rolling his eyes and chuckled. "You said you need my number again?" he sipped his drink.

"Yep, I lost my cell."

"What happened?" Gustavo anticipated an elaborate ruse with his firstborn emerging as a tragic hero figure.

"It had had its day."

"Come on, it's only six months old!"

There was a silence as his son decided what to say next. "Well, let's just say it wasn't waterproof."

It was Gustavo's turn to roll his eyes. He told him his phone number and then, "but I'm not getting you a new phone. You have to look after your things a lot better than that."

"It was an accident!" the boy pleaded.

63

"Even if that's the case, I'm not getting you another one. They don't grow on trees, you know."

The exchange might have gone on longer but Rosa cleared her throat, reminding him she was there. He cut the conversation short, said good-bye, and hung up. Gustavo prepared himself a refill but with some revisions to his original recipe. This time he poured the rum for longer and used less coke. He opened one of the kitchen drawers. Almost hidden under a box of 9mm ammo was a pack with diamond-shaped light blue pills.

Believing in the importance of first impressions, he used the pills the first time he was with a woman. He took a pill from the blister and washed it down with his drink. He did this so fast he felt sure Rosa did not even notice.

He walked to the sofa and sat next to Rosa. Her white mini skirt strained to cover the appropriate parts. He let his hand rest on her leg. It felt silky smooth to his touch. She had killer legs, and favored skirts that showed them to advantage. At five-six, she made up her height with a perfect classic Coca-Cola bottle shape.

"You seem to be on good terms with your ex-wife." He detected a trace of annoyance in her voice.

"Yeah, well. She is the mother of my children. Besides, I wasn't a good husband."

"Really?"

"You see, I have a problem. I'm a lesbian."

Rosa arched her eyebrow, "Really?"

"I am a lesbian," he repeated, "because I only sleep with women," he said with a straight face.

She laughed when she got the joke. "Aren't you eating?" She was almost done with her sandwich.

"I'm not hungry right now." He sipped from his drink and continued caressing her leg.

She took the last bite, washed it down with the last gulp of her Coke and gave him an inviting smile, her honey-colored eyes twinkling. She took his hand and led him to the bedroom.

Rosa stopped by the bed. Gustavo kissed the back of her neck. His hands stroked up and down the contours of her hips and waist. She moaned as he sucked on her earlobe. He unbuttoned her navy blue blouse. She moved her shoulders and the blouse slid down her arms and fell to the floor. Gustavo walked around the bed to the opposite wall. He turned on the air conditioner unit and came back to face her. Her face was partially visible in the moonlight filtering through the window. He studied her long legs, trim waist, and narrow shoulders. Her statuesque figure reminded him of a marble statue, with beauty equaling those adorning fountains in Rome.

She pulled his polo shirt over his head and undid the button of his Dockers twill pants. When he pulled down the zipper, the pants fell down.

She took a step back, smiled, and said, "I think my blouse coming off was sexier than your pants falling down."

He laughed, nodded, and said, "Ah, but I have something for you that stays up, so if you will just lie down ..."

* * * *

Gustavo spread the contents of the folder on top of the coffee table in front of him. He took the remote and turned on the TV set. He changed channels until he found music videos that appealed to him and set the volume low, so as not to disturb Rosa who was fast asleep and then he dropped the remote on the sofa beside him. He unwrapped his sandwich and read while he ate, taking in bits of information and bites of food at the same time.

The file was pretty straightforward. Miguel Delgado, aged twelve, drowned while vacationing at a beachfront hotel in Puerto Cortés. Gustavo stopped reading, his mind drifting off. What would it be like to bury a son? The thought alone was unbearable.

He remembered his agony in the hospital hallway a couple of years before, when doctors fought to save his son's legs after a car had run him over. When the medic came out with a jubilant smile on his face, it had been one of the peak moments in life as a father. The boy recovered in full; he even took to playing soccer again. But the ten or so hours he had sat outside, not knowing, biting his nails, praying, had been terrible unmitigated agony. He related to the father, pictured him burying the beloved son, only to have to deal with the insurance company later. Now the company wanted Gustavo to take a closer look at the claim.

He continued reading; all the documents complete and correct. What caught the attention of the clerk who processed the documentation was the birth certificate.

It stated the Delgado boy was born eight years earlier, not twelve. Gustavo frowned and thought that was weird. Not impossible, he had told Roger the truth on the phone earlier: many Hondurans registered late and, to avoid the ensuing late fees, lied about the birthday. The average was one or two years; a full four-year span was a bit unusual.

Of course, there were other reasons to have a later registration number. Living abroad and coming back into Honduras after many years, one is logged in the book at the time of registration. The registry officials do not provide addenda to old books. Gustavo read the birth certificate again. The birth was clearly marked for that year, not just issued then. That squashed his late registration theory.

Mr. Simmons had written on his e-mail that he wanted to avoid travel expenditure as much as possible, but considering the dubious paperwork, Gustavo figured a trip to Puerto Cortés was unavoidable.

CHAPTER THIRTEEN

DALLAS, TEXAS

Sebastian entered the dark bar with a single goal in mind: to get drunk.

The day's training session with Bill Knox had left him exhausted, but once he arrived at his hotel room, anxiety took hold of him. Bar fridges in hotel rooms were nothing but overpriced temptation. The two tiny bottles lasted two gulps apiece. They did nothing for him. Kelly and Joshua still appeared every time he closed his eyes. He stormed out of his room, desperate to find oblivion.

He hesitated at the entrance. A friend from the FDNY had told him about this place. Dallas firefighters comprised the majority of its patrons. The bar reeked of beer and cigarette smoke. Amusing how people, who made a living putting out fires, lit up as soon as their shift ended. He'd quit smoking after Kelly had given birth to Joshua. Damn! When would everything stop reminding him of them? Then again, he didn't want to forget he was once happy, part of something special. He willed his legs to move.

After navigating through busy pool tables, taking care to walk behind the guys playing darts, he sat at the bar. The stools on either side held large dudes. He had to sit sideways and ended up wedged shoulder-to-shoulder when he faced the bar.

Before he lost his family, he'd go to such bars to enjoy a quiet couple of beers to unwind from the trials of the day. The bar patrons in Dallas seemed to be doing the same. The bartender took his order and a vodka on ice materialized within a minute. At least the service was fast.

"I need a card if you want to run a tab," the bartender said.

Sebastian placed a fifty-dollar-bill on the counter top. "Tell me when this runs out."

He gulped the crystal clear liquid and savored the sweet scent, followed by the bitter taste. He signaled the bartender for a refill.

After the second drink arrived, the guy on his right said, "Hope you're not driving, pal."

"Back off."

"Listen, I'm with the fire department," the man said. "You know what I did before coming here? I pried the top half of a man out of a driver's seat. The car kept the bottom half."

"Mind your own business, will you?" He had taken such calls, too.

"He was drunk." The man continued as if he hadn't heard Sebastian. "I don't want to have to do that twice in the same evening."

"You wouldn't anyway. Unless in Dallas they let you guys drink while on duty." He nodded toward the beer.

The man stood up. "I'm off duty!"

"Then relax and let me be."

"You're going too fast with that vodka." He pointed at the half-empty glass.

"So?"

"Do you have a car?"

"None of your business."

"I'll make it my business."

Sebastian sipped from his drink.

"I asked if you had a car."

"And I told you it's none of your damn business."

"I am—"

"You're so full of shit. You come to drink and won't let me do the same." He finished the drink and signaled the bartender for a refill.

The bartender hesitated. He looked nervous and glanced at the standing man who shook his head.

"I'm warning you." The man lifted a finger to the bartender.

"I'm a paying customer. He's not even the freaking manager." Turning to the bartender, he said, "I'll sue your ass if you don't bring me a drink."

Sebastian had had bar brawls before, but never on such stupid grounds. He stood up and realized the man was as broad shouldered as him, but not as tall. Sebastian towered over him by almost half a foot. He felt sorry he had quit cigarettes. It would have given him immense pleasure to blow smoke in the prick's face.

The bartender's demeanor made it plain that a fight was the last thing he wanted inside his establishment. He kept looking from one man to the other, uncertain. Then he took a deep breath and nodded. He served ice, poured vodka, a double measure, and left the drink on the counter top.

Sebastian looked at the drink, and realized it was in a plastic cup. The bartender placed a top over it. He had to smile; the smart bastard was telling him to take it outside. "This one is on the house." He took the fifty-dollar bill and made the change.

Sebastian grabbed the drink. He left the money on the counter top. "Get him another beer."

"I don't want your freaking beer."

Sebastian expected the man to grab the money and throw it at his face. "Ah, shut up. Go fetch a cat off a tree or something."

With the parting shot, and his drink for the road, he walked out. He felt eyes on his back all the way to the door. He kept a firm stride, forcing himself to look ahead, fighting the urge to look back.

When he was on the sidewalk, he turned left and reached the corner where he flagged down a cab. Car or no car, he would not give the sonofabitch the satisfaction of admitting he was not driving tonight.

CHAPTER FOURTEEN

SAN PEDRO SULA, HONDURAS

Marcos lowered the window and took the ticket the guard at the shopping mall entrance handed him and passed it to Manuel. The rain did not stop the absurd security system; the guard stood looking like a giant yellow condom in his waterproof poncho. The ticket was a hard plastic rectangular token, decorated with colorful graphics and the mall's logo, big and imposing, in the center. Some drops of rain found their way inside the edge of the window but Marcos powered it up fast.

"What car are we looking for?" Manuel asked.

He chose Manuel over Pablo to accompany him today for two reasons. Although Pablo was smarter, his tattoos and mania for ripped shirts made him conspicuous and Marcos knew the shopping mall had video surveillance. Manuel was large, but looked like any ordinary overweight Honduran.

"A Toyota Tundra, a model not older than two years. You look on the right and I'll check the left."

"Okay." Manuel turned to check the parked cars while Marcos drove at 10kmh, as if looking for a space.

The other reason for his selection was character; Pablo had a temper that challenged every iota of Marcos's self-control, while Manuel was more equable.

Their slow navigation, earned some angry honks. A man even flipped him a finger as he passed him by. In response, Marcos changed the radio station. He continued pushing the pre-programmed buttons until he found a station playing bachatas, his favorite genre; he hummed to the tune as he continued to scan for his prey.

When they completed one full circle around the parking lot, Marcos swore under his breath.

"Tundras are not popular anymore," Manuel commented.

Marcos did not intend giving up. More often than not, it paid off to make these hunting trips. On occasions, though, they turned out to be duds but he decided to wait it out. He saw an empty spot and parked the car.

"Let's get something to drink."

They spent half an hour window-shopping in the mall, sodas in their hands. The crowd left little room; if the parking lot was bumper to bumper, the halls were shoulder to shoulder. People escaping from the heat took to the malls. The untrained eye might think the businesses were raking in the money, but Marcos knew better. He counted the people holding shopping bags and had fingers to spare in one hand. The majority of the mall's population was made up of teenagers, horsing around or walking while texting on their cellular phones.

Nowadays, few people walked with their heads held high looking where they were walking. He hated the darn things, and only after strict orders from Howard had he begun to carry a mobile. Not that it helped, because he kept forgetting to charge it, much to his boss's chagrin.

"Time to go." He tossed the empty plastic bottle into the trash.

They walked out and watched a red Tundra pass in front of them. Marcos traded a look with Manuel, a smile pasted on his face. They veered to the right, following the truck, in the opposite direction from where they had parked.

The driver found a free parking spot. A man in his mid-twenties got out. As he walked away, he aimed the remote over his shoulder and the car beeped as the taillights blinked once.

Marcos and Manuel walked past the car. Marcos turned in time to see the man entering the mall.

"You have the ticket?"

In reply, Manuel pulled it out of his back pocket. Marcos nodded, pleased, and tilted his head toward the car. "I'll keep watch."

Manuel went to the driver's door, looked around as he pulled something out of his pocket. Marcos knew it was a small set of tools, including the stick that Carlos had already programmed for recent model Tundra trucks. He admitted a third reason for choosing Manuel: his proficiency at hot-wiring cars. In less than ten seconds, he'd opened the door and stepped in. The alarm blared out. Marcos watched all around as Manuel ducked under the dashboard.

The alarm going off did not attract the guards. He looked at the gate, half-expecting to see the owner come back with the control in his hand. He counted the seconds as he envisioned Manuel ripping the cables under the dashboard, connecting the two correct ones with the small pliers to bypass the alarm and switching it on. The trick worked like a charm. The alarm stopped. The taillights blinked twice. A second later, the engine started, the reverse lights came on, and Manuel backed out. Twenty-three seconds.

Manuel passed him by, not stopping or waving, and turned toward the exit. That had been the plan. They had anticipated cameras in the parking lot and taken precautions. He lowered the flap of his baseball cap. Marcos reached the corner in time to see Manuel handing out the token to the guard before speeding out.

He smiled when the guard took no heed of the car or its driver.

Marcos returned to his vehicle. Careful to leave by a different exit from the one he used to enter, he approached the guard and lowered the window.

"I'm sorry. I lost the ticket."

The guard did not look pleased. "What?"

"I went to the bathroom. You know, when you gotta go, you gotta go." He did his best to look apologetic.

The downpour had increased in the last few minutes. Drops splashed against the armrest inside the car door. Marcos looked at the water, then at the guard, hoping he conveyed that he was sorry, but also worried about the car. The guard sighed.

"Show me the car registration and your driver's license."

He complied without delay and presented a registration card Carlos had prepared, with the owner's name matching the license. In any fast examination, the car belonged to Marcos.

The guard took a cursory look but did not even write it down. "The token costs fifty Lempiras."

"That's steep!" He did not want to appear too willing to pay, just in case.

"Don't lose it and you won't pay for it, sir."

He shook his head, looking annoyed. He made a show of irritation as he pulled out his wallet, counted a few bills, and then handed the money to the guard.

The guard pocketed the bills, issued a nameless receipt and returned the documents to Marcos, and signaled him to leave.

Marcos left without thanking the guard. He was playing the part of the angry customer.

There are some things money can't buy, but he sure could get a flame red Toyota Tundra for fifty Lempiras. He thought of the token again: stupid security system!

Chapter Fifteen

Dallas, Texas

Sebastian knew he had been putting off this meeting for too long.

He had been in Dallas for about three weeks now, and was enjoying the new job, despite himself. He'd complicated his life somewhat by returning his rental. It was not optional; he couldn't afford to keep it any longer. Still, it had taken him some time to get used to public transportation.

In his brief time in the city, he had learned its rhythm. He no longer minded the constant country music playing on the radio. Roger Simmons had proved to be a good boss and William Knox one heck of a guy to learn from.

Going to the shrink was the tricky part. He avoided it as much as he could. James had called two days before with the whopping news, "You got an appointment!" His cheerful manner would have made anybody think it was a date with a hot girl.

After five minutes, Sebastian ran out of excuses. James, as he had since they were boys, had won again.

Sebastian wondered if James used that older-brother attitude with his wife. Nah, he concluded, Christine was the true ruler of the castle there. Sebastian had always had a soft spot for Christine. He'd liked her since the first time James had taken her to their parents' home for dinner. She understood her husband very well and knew how to run his numbers.

It was a shame she and Kelly had not got along. They'd behaved as though they hated each other, making family reunions very uncomfortable for everyone. Neither James nor Sebastian could determine the root cause of the animosity. They'd learned to cope with it, as did the wives who strained to maintain an environment of affability for their husbands, most of the time.

Yet, at the service for Kelly and Joshua, with the closed empty caskets, nobody cried as hard as Christine. They were not crocodile tears either he was sure. She'd been devastated. Sebastian assumed that a very worried Christine had orchestrated the little intervention dinner on his birthday. As a good puppeteer, she probably invented that PTA meeting so James would have to do the dirty work. Once Sebastian had bitten the hook, she had e-mailed him the hotel reservation the following morning. Yep, she was a devious but good-hearted she-devil.

Now, the latest step in the "let's mess with Sebastian's life" saga was to make sure he was referred to a psychologist in Dallas, the fabulous Patrick Jones, head doctor. The appointment was for Tuesday at two in the afternoon. "Be there, or be square," had been the edict. Great!

He sat in the reception area. The place had the same antiseptic smell typical of hospitals; he wondered why. The shrink's office back in the city always smelled of lavender.

"Mr. Martin? You may go in now." The receptionist, a girl who could not be older than eighteen, pointed him to the door.

The simple act of walking across the threshold felt ominous. He felt unprepared for what he would find inside. Doctor Jones's sanctum sanctorum looked nothing like James's office or that of Sebastian's last shrink. This place looked like a living room, a bachelor's living room. He smelled the elegant aroma of leather couches facing each other. A round marble-top coffee table occupied most of the space between them. A roll top desk stood at the far end. It looked as though it belonged in a Humphrey Bogart movie. The doctor stood, and brought down the panel, covering his laptop from prying eyes. He wore a formal dark gray suit. A three-piece. Sebastian expected to see a gold chain tied to the last button of the vest and a pocket watch.

"Good afternoon, Mr. Martin." On closer examination, Dr. Jones wore a fine pinstripe.

Sebastian shook the doctor's hand and felt comforted by the firm grip. The doctor sat on one of the couches and gestured for Sebastian to sit across from him, a notebook and pen ready on the coffee table. He sat down with a sigh. Here we go again.

"Since this is our first meeting I'd like to cover some background information with you. Is that okay?" His tone was even, bordering on condescending. An affable smile never left his face.

Sebastian gave a noncommittal nod.

"Good." Dr. Jones took the notebook and read from his notes. "You were referred to me from New York. I see you are a distinguished member of the FDNY."

"That seems a thousand years ago."

"Just a bit over seven months have passed though."

"If you say so."

"Were you raised in New York?"

"The Bronx. I'm sure you've heard of my brother, James Martin."

"I may have." His tone sounded dismissive. "What was it like to grow up in the Bronx during the seventies?"

"It was okay, I guess. We heard first-hand gossip from Studio 54. I remember the summer of Sam, and the disco music."

"Interesting. All good themes for movie making." Sebastian heard palpable sarcasm. "That comes across as superfluous. I am sure you can dig deeper than that."

The doctor's gaze remained locked on him.

Sebastian felt like a bug under a microscope. Worse, the green eyes radiated intimidating energy, like laser beams. Despite the cold, Sebastian rubbed his sweaty hands on his pants. He sighed, then stood and paced around the room.

"I remember spending every afternoon with James. We played basketball or football." He smiled, remembering a particular incident. "I always made James know how hard I could tackle him. Even back then I outweighed him by ten pounds."

"I bet he didn't like that."

"Yeah, he always whined he preferred baseball. He was a decent hitter."

"Let's see," Dr. Jones turned a page from the notebook, "do you know why you are here?"

"I'm here because my brother is a pain in the butt and won't leave me alone."

"Really? Is that what you think of your brother?" Sebastian noted the serious expression that replaced the smile. "That he has nothing better to do than mess with your life?"

This surprised Sebastian. Taken aback by a comeback sounding so much like an open confrontation, he stopped pacing and remained quiet, without a smart quip or insult to shoot back.

"Let's look at a different angle." The doctor left the notebook and pen on the desk. "What do you expect to accomplish with our sessions?"

"You mean like goals?"

"Yes, why not? Let's set some goals."

The change in tactics took Sebastian off guard. He went back to the sofa, considering whether to walk out or not, only to realize he had already sat down. Maybe his subconscious was telling him something.

"Doctor Jones, I know you mean well. But listen, no

matter how much therapy I get, I'll never get my family back."

"I am relieved you're aware of that. But it is not the kind of goal I meant. Would you like, at least, to be able to cope with your loss?" he suggested.

Running a marathon could not have left him more spent than he felt at that moment. Why did people not understand he just wanted to be left the hell alone? "Does your little book," he pointed to the pad on the table, "tell you how my wife and son died?"

"Air accident."

"No gory details?" The doctor shook his head.

"'An accident' is such an understatement."

* * * *

An air pocket forced the 747 into a short plunge. A male voice filled the air through the P.A. "This is an emergency. All passengers, please return to your seats and fasten your seatbelts."

Sebastian Martin grabbed the armrests so hard his knuckles turned white before his left hand reached for his seat belt and found it already buckled. He never took it off except for nature calls or after landing. A seasoned fire fighter with the FDNY, he had seen crash sites and never felt comfortable inside planes.

He looked across the aisle at his wife, Kelly, and son, Joshua. He had to get a grip and not infect the eight-year-old with his fear. He checked his watch, not long to go.

The lights went out. A rumble grew louder and louder. He heard frightened screams from other passengers. A knot in the pit of his stomach told him they were about to plummet, then the force of gravity plastered him to the back of his seat. The oxygen masks dropped down from the bulkhead as dim emergency lights came on. With his mask in place, he turned to his right. Kelly had her mask on already and he watched as she helped Joshua. She pulled the white plastic strap, and then held their son's hand. After nine years of marriage, Sebastian and Kelly could communicate their thoughts with a single look: they didn't know if they'd make it out of there alive.

A flight attendant ran the length of the plane from the back. Even in the dim light, he recognized the fear in her eyes as she made sure everybody had buckled up. She had to shout above the deafening roar.

The plane rocked from side to side. A few of the overhead bins opened and luggage pieces bombarded the cabin. He deflected a duffle bag with his forearm. One of the bag's metal buckles nicked him and blood trickled down from the stinging scratch.

The noise increased. A massive tremor shook the plane and Sebastian feared the worst: the fuselage would collapse. The sound of ripping metal filled the cabin, overwhelming any scream.

He turned to his wife and saw her moving away. That's impossible, he thought. A tiny ray of daylight from above illuminated her. He heard a screeching sound as metal wrenched from metal, as the light increased and a section beside the wing broke away from the airliner.

With a sense of surreal lingering, an adagio that defied reality, he watched Kelly and Joshua sucked out then float away into the emptiness. They hung, suspended, in time, motion and the raw air.

His gaze locked on Kelly's face, her eyes wide with fear. All sound faded away. Through the clear plastic mask, he saw her mouth open. He couldn't hear her scream, but her voice was crystal clear in his ear. Clouds took their place as the plane raced to earth and left them to follow.

Through the gap, air rushed in, creating mayhem and devilry in its onslaught. Luggage, backpacks, shoes, cans, cups, the sick bags, and safety cards from the seat pockets, newspapers and magazines swirled, dipped and dived and danced, like a ticker tape parade, leaving Sebastian gasping from the icy air and smelling the fear all around him.

He ripped off the gas mask and cried out to the space where his family had been seconds before. His right hand stretched out to grasp them, his reflexes refusing to accept they were no longer there. He blinked hard. This had to be a nightmare. He felt a trickle on his cheek before he tasted the saltiness of tears mixed with his sweat.

His stomach contracted with the plane's rushed descent. He caught the stench of urine and excreta, mingling with the acrid smell of terror. They were going down; he'd join Kelly and Joshua very soon. He turned to the space they had vacated, begging for them to be there. Instead, he saw the hole across the aisle. He distinguished buildings. And water. Lots of water. The ocean.

His heart pumped so hard, he thought it would burst through his chest, trying to break free, like the creature in *Alien*. He had walked in and out of flaming structures of all kinds, houses, apartment buildings, office buildings, but this ungodly dread was new to him.

The aircraft leveled as it approached the ground. He talked himself through the instructions for an emergency landing. Like a black hole in space, anything not tied down continued to dance through the gap. Amidst the pandemonium in the main cabin, the pilot issued a muffled announcement. It surprised Sebastian that the P.A. system still worked. And yet, he could have been underwater for all the sense he could make of what he heard.

A couple to his left screamed in despair. He willed his hand to let go of the armrest and reach for them. He tugged the lady's arm and she faced him. He bent over, protecting his head with his arms while keeping an eye on the woman. She nodded, understanding, before she turned to her husband and they both bent over. He intended to start a ripple effect with other passengers noticing and following suit, like a Mexican wave in a stadium.

A glance to his right, through the hole, showed him the black asphalt of a runway. They had reached an airport! People pointed at the oncoming ground and screamed at the earth rushing toward them. Air whooshed through the hole. The plane bumped, announcing it had touched ground. Black smoke spiraled through the hole.

A new noise filled the air. The landing gear was not working. Friction alone slowed the aircraft. Another bump and the plane tilted to the left. An explosion shook the plane. Through the hole on his right he watched sparks spray from underneath. Another explosion and the flight came to an abrupt, jolting, end, bouncing Sebastian's head off the seat in front, his stomach taking strain from the seatbelt.

The emergency lights faded. More sweat broke from his forehead reminding him of something familiar. The temperature was rising. The firefighter in him took over. He unbuckled fast, took a deep breath before removing the mask, and looked around the plane.

One of the emergency exits was two rows behind him. He took another furtive look at the gap where his family had disappeared and saw grass not too far away.

He crossed to the exit door. On the seat next to it, a man wearing a business suit remained hunched over, as if frozen with fear, in the crash position.

"Sir, we need to open that door."

The man did not move. Sebastian tapped him on the back but the man did not respond. With no time to waste on pleasantries, Sebastian grabbed him by the collar to pull him up and realized the man had fainted. He clambered over the man, moved the lever, pulled inward, and slid it to the side. Above the screams of men, women and children filling the air, Sebastian heard a hiss as an inflatable slide rolled out and reached the ground.

Turning back to the unconscious man, Sebastian unlocked the seat belt and carried him out to an empty seat in another row. The man slumped to one side. Sebastian cursed at the delay.

The smoke made vision difficult and he blinked again repeatedly to clear his blurring vision and the tears. Every time he closed his eyes, he saw Kelly with her hand outstretched. He forced the image aside. He needed to concentrate on the other people on the plane; the ones with a chance to escape.

Alarms went off, the flight attendants screamed instructions to passengers frantic to exit the plane, who didn't give a shit about order or anyone else. They became an acephalic mob.

"Hey, the exit's over here!" he bellowed.

The authority he commanded was enough for a few doubtful heads to turn. He stood illuminated by the sunlight coming through the large hole. The couple who had been sitting to his left was the first to stand and follow his instructions.

"There is grass below, it'll be okay. Just slide, now!" he ordered. "Take off your shoes!"

The woman was about to jump when he held her arm.

"You go down first." He pointed at the mid-forties husband. "Then you catch her." The man nodded, pushed past his wife and went out.

As instructed, once down, the man turned with open arms to receive his wife. She took the step. After the couple, others rushed toward him, elbowing whoever was in their path and screaming for help. They almost toppled over Sebastian in their desperation to be next.

He raised his hands and yelled, "We need to calm down, people. Everyone will get out but in order."

His shouts shocked people into obedience, still terrified, but grateful they'd found a leader. His commanding height of over six feet, his booming voice, and his stance always made him perfect for that role.

"Women and children nearest here will go first." He thought of Kelly and Joshua – his woman and child. They had been the first to exit. He tried to swallow but his mouth had gone dry.

A thin woman wearing a silk dress stepped forward. He helped her to the edge. She looked at the couple on the ground as if calculating her next step. She sighed and then turned around. He thought she had changed her mind but then she bent down and removed her stiletto-heeled shoes. She gave him an apologetic smile and faced the edge again. This time she took a deep breath, sat on the slide and slid out.

Next in line was a plump, elderly lady. Her faced showed horror at the prospect of jumping off. Thinking on his feet, he pulled a broad-shouldered man forward and placed him beside the woman. They slid down together. When she tried to get up, the woman's knees collapsed and she rolled to the ground, but the man rushed to help her.

Sebastian coughed from the black smoke filling the cabin. He worried one exit would not be enough to evacuate the entire plane in time. Standing on the edge, Sebastian looked to the front of the airplane and saw with relief another exit slide, with passengers already moving out.

He went back and strived to move the line of people faster. Some were injured; a man had fashioned a sling out of his own shirt, another held a bloody rag to his forehead. A woman's nose, red and bulging, he deduced must be broken.

His spirits rose a bit when he heard the familiar fire truck siren. It had always amazed him how people would greet firemen arriving at an emergency call with relief plain on their faces, some even embracing total strangers.

This was the first time he'd been on the other side and now he understood why. Firemen in full gear rushed out of the moving trucks to help the people already out of the plane.

His mind hurtled back to Joshua and Kelly. Kelly's silenced scream, her eyes. Always a man of action in time of danger, he'd failed when the time came to save his own family. The plane had still been flying over water when he last saw them. He thought of hitting the water with such velocity from that altitude ... and what it would have done to their bodies. Like rag dolls hitting a concrete wall. He had seen the aftermath of such cases.

"Sir, can you help me?"

A woman carrying a baby tugged at Sebastian's arm. He pushed the vivid images out of his mind. He had a job to do here and now. He cleared his eyes with the back of his hand, making them sting even more. He blinked fast for a second, then focused on the woman and child.

Without a word, he took the baby. Sensing a stranger, the baby emitted a piercing cry. The woman sat down on the edge of the slide and stretched her arms, demanding her treasure back. The moment the baby felt the mother, warm again, the crying stopped. She cooed for an instant. Sebastian gave her a gentle push and they slid down.

The line continued to move until only a female flight attendant remained in line.

"Sir, you need to go now," she said.

He shook his head. "People still in the front?"

"Other crew members are seeing to them. We need to leave now."

"Hold on." He found the man he had carried away from the emergency door slumped where he had left him, still unconscious. He carried him toward the exit and lay him down on the edge of the slide.

"You need to go with him," he told the attendant.

"I can't. You have to go with him."

85

Of course, she would say that, trained to act responsibly in case of an emergency. Sebastian could not leave the aircraft yet; something forced him to stay. A gut feeling that sliding off the plane would seal the fate of his family. He shook his head.

"Not yet." He picked up the attendant, placed her near the door. Then a gentle push was enough for her to lose balance and slide down.

Now he was the only one at the door. But he wasn't sure he was alone onboard. He looked again through the door and saw people still going out through the front exit.

He looked around the cabin one last time and walked toward the front exit. He passed by the gap and now he realized three full rows were missing. He hadn't noticed anyone else pulled out of the plane. He closed his eyes and the images of crushed bodies, his family, returned. He lost track of time as he stood rooted on the spot.

"Kelly, Joshua," he whispered and let the tears fall, unable to contain them any longer. He sat on his seat, the spot was important to him: it was where he had last seen them. He stretched out his hand toward the hole.

He saw beyond the charred grass and fire fighters busy with the flames, beyond the passengers being evacuated, beyond the clouds and the sky and all the way to where he saw nothing but the faces of Kelly and Joshua. Without them, he had no reason to continue living.

He had trouble breathing. He didn't care if it were due to the smoke. He only knew he felt a crushing, intense, physical, pressure on his chest. He welcomed it. He wanted to join his family.

The plane shook a little and brought him back to reality. He felt somebody tugging at his sleeve and turned to see another flight attendant prompting him to move.

Like an automaton, he followed her to the front exit.

"It's your turn now, sir," said the man wearing a white

shirt with the captain's insignia.

Looking at the captain's swollen hands resurrected the firefighter in him. He grabbed the stewardess by the arms and almost threw her out.

"Need help jumping off?" he motioned toward the captain's hands.

"I'm all right. Go, I'll follow," he said.

"Come on, it's not time to sink with the ship," Sebastian pointed out and the captain acknowledged him with half a smile.

As if on cue, both men jumped out from the flaming aircraft.

* * * *

"I didn't see Joshua."

"What do you mean?" Doctor Jones asked.

"When the seats broke apart, I only saw Kelly."

"From your point of view, the boy was behind Kelly. She blocked your line of sight."

A moment of silence.

"You didn't forget about him, Sebastian. Neither have you proved that you loved her more than you loved him."

"When I saw pictures afterwards, the plane looked as if Godzilla had taken a big chunk out of it. When we boarded the plane and realized my seat was across the aisle, I raised hell. Stupid newbie at the check-in counter messed it up." Sebastian felt spent.

"Have you considered that her mistake saved your life?"

"You call *this* a life? I would have preferred to die with them." Then something occurred to him. Looking down, he added, "Or instead of them."

"Are you sure about that? Would you have wanted them to go through your suffering?"

He looked up at the doctor and felt ashamed of his last statement. He was cornered. How could he desire such a miserable life for his wife and kid? He felt dazed. "Don't I love them anymore?" His heart pounded, and he heard his heartbeat echo in his ears.

"Mr. Martin. It is not that you don't love them anymore. You're just tired of feeling miserable. Believe me when I tell you, this might actually be a good thing."

"What?" The idea felt preposterous.

"It might be the sign that you are ready to deal with your issues."

"Hit rock bottom?"

Doctor Jones nodded. "And bounce back."

"I—"

The doctor cut him off. "No, don't try to figure it out. That's my job." The doctor gave him a benevolent smile.

"My time is up?"

He looked at his wristwatch. "Five minutes left. But today I'll let you go early. It may improve your desire to continue with the sessions."

"The real money is in extended treatment and not in one-shot visits, right?"

Exploding in laughter, Dr. Jones shed all pretenses. He stood up and put out his hand.

Sebastian rose, shook his hand and left. Every time he'd left the doctor's office in New York, he'd left with different levels of anger, depending on the subject matter of each session. This time he went out feeling ambivalent, and that was a first. He was not sure how he felt about it.

He stood in the anteroom and thought of something that made him smile. It was a movie. A character's line that echoed his feeling.

"So what if this is as good as it gets?" he said to no one in particular.

"Well," a female voice said, "you're not Jack Nicholson."

CHAPTER SIXTEEN

DALLAS, TEXAS

Sebastian sat across the small round table from Jill Simmons. They were at a Starbucks half a block down from Doctor Jones's office.

"How do you like Dallas so far?"

"It's okay, I guess." He shrugged. "Big change from New York."

"Yes, it is."

"Have you ever been to New York?"

"Went to college there, spent four years riding the subways." She chuckled and for a second seemed lost in thought, probably reliving a particular memory. She turned serious.

Remembering her reaction at the BBQ, Sebastian figured she had remembered something about the ex-husband. She remained quiet. He racked his brain for a change of topic as the sound of the busy coffee house filled the void of their uncomfortable silence.

"I think Dallas is great in its own way. I've met lots of good people," he said.

"Give it some time, you haven't been here long enough," she said. "How are you getting along with Bill?" She cradled her cup between her hands, and took sips every now and then.

Relieved at the reprieve, Sebastian told her about Bill's teaching. He even mentioned a few particulars from cases, careful to omit names. She asked very probing questions, asking for more specific details on certain situations. They managed to stay away from touchy subjects. He told her about his life as a fireman. Then they hit another blank.

Jill looked down at her cup, her hands playing around it. Sebastian smiled. He thought he knew what was on her mind.

"Go ahead, you can ask me about nine eleven."

She looked up with a frown.

"The subject always comes up when people learn I used to be in the FDNY."

"Were you there?"

He nodded.

"On the day it happened?"

Sebastian nodded again.

"I heard the department lost people." Her voice trailed off.

"Three hundred and forty three from the Fire Department alone, including a Commissioner and a Chief of the Department."

"Wow," was all she could mutter. "Did you ..." She couldn't finish. The worry lines on her forehead deepened.

"... know any of them?" he concluded and she nodded.

"All of them." After a small pause he added, "I had helped an office clerk out when they told me to stay put."

Once again, he felt the same sense of impotence, of being there and not accomplishing anything. Lost in his memory, unsure for how long, it dawned on him that yet another awkward silence surrounded them.

He looked at her. She held her head tilted, her lips curved into a benevolent and knowing smile. At any other time, he would have reacted to her pity but now, he looked down instead.

CHAPTER SEVENTEEN

PUERTO CORTÉS, HONDURAS

The digital clock on the dashboard of Gustavo's car marked a quarter to noon. Up ahead, a large overhead white sign with bold black letters announced the end of the highway that connected San Pedro Sula to Puerto Cortés. After driving under the sign, Gustavo Fonseca had crossed into the city limits. Other than that, the road showed no change.

He passed a few industrial buildings on his right, knew the Caribbean white sand beach was about a mile behind them. He turned down the aircon and rolled down the windows to let the salty coastal air wash all over him.

Approaching an overpass that headed toward the port city of Omoa, he turned to the right. Commercial and residential buildings appeared, no higher than two stories, cramped together on both sides of the road. He made a hard left, then straight ahead to stop for a red light.

He had come to Puerto Cortés on countless occasions, for both business and pleasure. Not only did the city hold the largest seaport facility in Central America, at thirty miles from San Pedro Sula, it was the closest place to spend sunny Sundays at the beach. There were several above-average restaurants specializing in sea-food, making the drive for lobster or the traditional deep-fried fish with plantain chips a frequent getaway for lunch, even on weekdays.

Today, however, he did not make the forty-five minute drive for the tempting delicacies, or to get a tan. It did not matter how appetizing the aromas, or pleasing the gentle waves that seemed to call to him. This trip was for business.

The light changed to green. It was not hard to find one's way around the city, the core laid out as it was in a grid pattern. He knew where he needed to go and after a few turns he parked in front of a two-story, green wooden building, another legacy of the banana company that used to run the port and railroad, built to service the industry in their prime, but that prime was the first half of the previous century. The beginning of the end started with a nationwide strike in 1954. The outcome included legislation to protect the employees, still valid to this day.

He climbed the stairs two at a time and entered a makeshift reception area, where a uniformed soldier sat behind a plain small secretarial desk.

"I'm looking for Lieutenant Moya."

"Who's calling?" The soldier's reply was crisp and straight.

"Gustavo Fonseca." He figured the boy to be a new recruit, the type who performs menial duties with life-threatening importance. Gustavo thought it sad that this eagerness was lost before the young men reached important ranks where it could make a difference.

"Lieutenant Moya is out of the office."

Gustavo frowned. "Are you sure?" He had called ahead.

"Yes, sir."

He took his phone out and dialed, he waited a few seconds for the connection to get through.

"*Hola*, Ricardo. Yes, I am here. No? I'll come out then." He pocketed the phone and waved goodbye to the receptionist before he left.

Gustavo Fonseca found Ricardo Moya just outside the building. The military man looked puzzled as he patted his pockets. "Got a cigarette?" he said as a greeting.

"Nope. Quit smoking last year. You should do the same."

"Nah. One lousy ad saying it gives cancer and everybody panics. Bunch of sissies, if you ask me. Walk with me."

They walked together about half a block down the street to a vendor stand, the type the vendor packed up and took home every night. A simple four by two table, every inch of the top covered with products that included cigarettes, matches, candies and gums.

"One pack of Belmont Blue, please."

With one swift motion, the vendor pulled the pack out of the display, handed it to Moya and took the money. The two men made small talk on the way back while Moya hit one end of the pack against his palm a few times.

"So, what's the kid's name?" He asked as he lit up.

"Miguel Delgado. He died on May second."

"That's the day after the Labor Day holiday."

"Yep."

"Hmm. OK, let's check that file."

Twenty minutes later, they were sitting inside Ricardo Moya's small office. He closed the door for privacy, as it was not permitted to show official files to civilians without court orders. Even to former military men.

However, when a man had been under fire in real combat situations, a special bond was established with those fighting by your side. Gustavo took advantage of such rapport whenever he could, but only as part of his job.

Besides, he always repaid in kind. When Ricardo's wife crashed her old beaten Corolla against a recent model Mercedes the previous year, Gustavo supervised the process. He made sure the workshop did not charge more than they should, that they repaired where they could and only made replacements when needed. Moya had been grateful; he had saved a lot of money because Gustavo had watched his back. The repayment of such small favors was how any good friendship worked.

"It reads here your boy Delgado died by drowning at a hotel by the beach. Poor family ... come for vacation and end up with a tragedy."

Gustavo nodded. "Very sad. Who made the call?"

"From the local hospital, it doubles up as a morgue. They have to report all deaths, shot wounds, anything. You know the drill."

"Yes, I know." Gustavo sighed. "Did they perform an autopsy?"

"No. The boy was dead on arrival at the hospital but they tried to revive him. The hospital only performs the autopsy when they are not sure about the cause of death."

"Operational cost?"

Moya smiled. "You got it." He looked up from the file. "What's next? You want to talk to the doctor?"

"Wouldn't hurt."

"I'll take you there."

Moya drove them in his official car. They arrived at a public hospital. Gustavo looked at the walls in need of paint, proof that the government ran the facility. The usual smell of antiseptic was present. The place was packed queues everywhere, with women in labor, others carrying children with running noses or allergies, people in wheelchairs, others leaning again the walls, all waiting patiently to see a doctor. Gustavo caught sight of a man in his mid-thirties holding a bloody handkerchief wrapped around his left hand. He held something in the other hand. Gustavo deduced he might be a construction worker with a severed finger.

Moya led him past the entrance to the nurses' station. The uniform helped to get quick responses from clerks and within minutes, they were talking with the doctor who had worked the shift the night of the accident. The man looked no more than a couple of years out of school. The dark shadows under his eyes spoke of night shifts or late night studying. A black stethoscope hung around his neck. He walked with the brisk pace typical of those running late for everything. They caught him on the go. Gustavo briefed him, and fired off his questions for fear the doctor would disappear in haste any second.

"Yes, I remember the boy. Tragic loss."

"Do you remember how old he was?"

"No, it should be on the file though."

"We will get the file on the way out," promised Moya.

"Was he the average size for an eight-year-old?" Gustavo insisted.

The doctor raised an eyebrow, as if the question seemed an odd one to ask. "Not unless he suffered elephantiasis. I think he was eleven or twelve, tops."

"Are you sure?"

"Of course I'm sure. You never forget those who died on your table." The doctor looked offended.

"I thought the boy was dead on arrival." Gustavo gave Moya a quizzical look.

"Regardless, we fought hard to bring him back!" The doctor snapped.

"Sorry, Doctor. I meant no offense. It's just that a few things don't add up."

"Cheapskate insurance bastards! Just pay the policy, damn it!" With that last shot, the doctor left.

"Gustavo, is there something you are not telling me?"

"I can't tell you."

"Don't give me that crap! I did not have to show you

my file or drag my butt here so that man," he pointed at the back of the doctor walking away, "could insult you."

"All right, all right." Gustavo raised his hands. He sighed then added, "the birth certificate the parents presented states the boy was eight years old."

Moya gave a low whistle as the implications dawned on him. "You think the doctor might be up to something?"

Gustavo pondered the question a moment before answering. "No, I don't think so. His reaction when I asked about the boy's size seemed pretty natural. Had he been in on it, he would not have said it like that."

"Where does that leave you, elephantiasis?"

"Hard to believe, isn't it?"

CHAPTER EIGHTEEN

DALLAS, TEXAS

"So, what's up for today?" Sebastian entered the office. Bill Knox was already behind his desk.

"Scams." Bill did not turn from his monitor.

"Really?"

"Yep." He pointed to a pile of papers on top of Sebastian's desk. "Read those. They're not insurance claims, just things I've picked up from here and there. Get back to me when you're done."

Taking his position behind the desk, Sebastian started with the first page from the top of the pile. He read in silence. The room echoed with the gentle but steady tapping from Bill's keyboard. An hour later, the tall stack had split into two smaller piles of about the same height.

"They do get creative," Sebastian observed about the content of a letter he had just finished reading.

"Yes. I was afraid to show that particular one to you."

The letter, or rather printed e-mail, allegedly came from a senior bank officer in some African country seeking assistance in collecting the money from an account. The account holder had died in an airliner accident a couple of years before.

According to the letter, the man died before appointing any beneficiary and the bank was about to foreclose the account and seize the funds. To prevent this, and earn something on the side, the bank officer claimed to have researched several databases until coming across a suitable candidate. The fact that the e-mail recipient and the deceased had the same last name was a plus.

The deal was simple; the bank officer would appoint the e-mail recipient as beneficiary, do the proper paperwork, and claim the funds from the account. After that, they would split them fifty-fifty. A sweet deal all around. Sebastian figured the fact that the proposal was outright illegal to begin with, only made it more tempting to potential victims.

"Because of the airplane crash?"

"Yes. They do their homework. I Googled that flight number and found news clips about the accident from respectable sources. In fact, it was all over the news the day it happened. So if you made a quick check …"

"You think it is possible?" Sebastian concluded.

"Exactly."

"And some people fall for this?" Sebastian could not believe people were so gullible in this day and age.

"Sure, all the time. There are several variations of the letter, like winning an electronic lottery you never heard of, or the survivor of a recently toppled dictatorship trying to sneak the money out of the country, or such as this."

"So what's the catch?"

"After a few e-mail exchanges, when the poor bastard is hooked, they drop the news that in order to move the funds they need to cover some expenses or fees."

"Can't they be deducted from the funds?"

"That would be the common sense approach, but then they sweet-talk you about the many reasons why that can't be done."

"Let me guess, after you send the money you never hear from them again?"

"Bingo!"

"You mean lottery?"

Although Bill laughed at that, Sebastian understood what his mentor tried to convey: never take anything at face value. This exercise was not within their realm of work but was a good illustration of what to expect.

"This afternoon I go to Roger's office. We meet once a week. Today will be my last. Starting next week I'm delegating the task to you."

"What? I don't think ..."

"Hell! If I don't push you out of the nest you'll never fly, boy!"

CHAPTER NINETEEN

SAN PEDRO SULA, HONDURAS

Reynaldo Puerto had big plans for tonight. Tired of teachers banging on about hormones and testosterone, he couldn't care less; he just wanted to get laid. At the moment, he lay on his bed. He was a month shy of eighteen years old and thought of the night ahead.

The closest he had gotten so far was two years ago. He had gone to study with a classmate. Following unrelenting persistence that bordered on harassment, she had agreed to go to her bedroom. When he thought they'd had enough foreplay, he unbuttoned the top of her blouse. Her father had walked in, shotgun in hand, and thrown him out of the house. The next day, the girl had begged him not to return. After eyeing the shotgun, Reynaldo didn't need telling twice.

But tonight he and his pal Jorge planned to visit one of the most popular strip clubs in San Pedro Sula. He'd get some even if he had to pay for it. There was no shame in that.

A *ding* on his computer brought him out of his reverie. He jumped from the bed and stomped on something that stung his foot.

He lifted his bare foot and saw the plastic controller of his game console. "Damn!"

As he hopped one-footed the rest of the way to the desk, Reynaldo grabbed the waistband of his oversized faded jeans and pulled them back up. The only thing preventing them from falling down completely was the two-inch black leather belt. He sat and looked at the screen. It was an instant message from Jorge. He read it and replied, typing in fury. What happened?

The answer appeared in the form of green letters on the screen: My mom crashed the car.

Their plans depended on the car.

Reynaldo: How about your father's?

Jorge: He said he needed it. btw mom is ok.

Reynaldo: Oops. Sorry. Glad she is fine.

They chatted a few moments longer, exploring other options. Arriving at the club by taxi, then taking the girls out to the motel, and grabbing a cab ride back home cost more money than they had. Even between them, they could not afford it. Reynaldo ran a hand through his disheveled black hair. He racked his brain to think of a way to find extra money.

His single mother worked as a loan officer for a car dealer. Her salary was enough to pay for his schooling, housing, and food. He had already received his monthly allowance. That well was empty. His father had left ten years ago to start another family. The father-son relationship amounted to a phone call around Christmas time, as neither of them cared to remember the other's birthday.

Although he knew how to drive, he could not get a license until the age of eighteen, so his strict mother would not lend him the car until then.

He was still pacing the room like a caged animal when his mother knocked on the door.

"Are you okay?"

"Yes. I'm fine." He spat out the words.

"If you say so. I'm going to the movies with Gina. Want to come?"

"No, thanks." He'd rather die before being caught at a theater with his mother and her friend.

The sound of a horn reached the room.

"That must be her. We might go for a drink afterwards."

"Great. Just go."

She shut the door, then popped her head again. "There is pizza in the oven. You better have something to eat before you go out."

"We're gonna have a blast," he said in a bitter tone.

His mother closed the door again, but this time she did not return.

Twenty minutes and two slices of pizza later, the phone rang. It was Jorge. Both of them sulked about their botched hunting excursion. Reynaldo sat on the couch, put his feet on the coffee table, something he would have not done if his mother were around. Looking at nothing in particular, as one does when on the phone, his gaze roamed around, until it came to rest on a particular spot.

A plate hung next to the front door. It had been a gift from his mother's colleague last Christmas. A row of five small hooks made a straight line across, beneath a picture of the Maya Ruins in Copan. Several key chains hung from there. One in particular caught his attention. On the center hook hung a key with a thick black base with two buttons.

"Mom left her car keys."

Her position in the company justified a preferential rate so she could afford a recent model car. Reynaldo knew the sacrifices she had to make every month to make ends meet. Lucky for her, the job also provided an allowance for gas. The Japanese four-door came with an efficient four-cylinder engine. It could almost run on thin air.

"So what? You're too chicken to take that green machine out," Jorge taunted.

Some time ago when Jorge spent the weekend there,

102

Reynaldo had refused to take his mother's car out for a spin. After that, the constant teasing on his lack of courage was making a dent in the teenager's pride.

"Tonight is different."

"You mean it?" The excitement plain in his tone.

"Yes, but you have to pay for gas."

"Sure."

"See you in ten." Reynaldo hung up and rushed to his room to change. The night was promising again.

* * * *

The Pachanga was the hottest new joint on the Twelfth Avenue, right in the heart of the area known as Zona Viva. In the late eighties, the city council organized a carnival, closing several streets and running nationwide commercials with the sound bite. The name stuck. Nowadays, the area expanded to several other avenues and comprised many restaurants, bars, and casinos. During the month of June, the street concerts were still customary as part of the city's anniversary.

Cruising at parade speed, Reynaldo couldn't find any parking space. His friend scanned the street, but the elusive jackpot took its toll.

"You should have parked back there."

"You can't park in front of a garage gate! Besides, it was two blocks away."

"It's late!"

Reynaldo grunted in response. He found a spot between a Ford Ranger and a new Beetle. It was just wide enough for his mother's Nissan sedan to fit, but he managed to squeeze in.

"I'll be damned. Parallel parking does work," commented Jorge.

They got out and crossed the street. They grumbled about the steep entry fee, but one look at the armed doorman, a scar running along his left cheek, made them think better of it and they complied.

The club was poorly illuminated; the low ceiling felt oppressive, the air heavy with the smoke from several hundred cigarettes. The last notes of a popular merengue tune died away as a new song faded in, this time reggae.

Reynaldo saw a flight of stairs going up to a balcony. He led Jorge through the people, and they went up to the balcony where the ceiling felt even lower but had fewer people. Reynaldo figured that, with girls dancing, the best places were next to the dance floor; but a table there demanded a required consumption. He had heard a full bottle of liquor was the minimum price.

They sat at a small round table overlooking the dance floor below. The waitress, a short plump woman wearing a denim skirt, approached them. Reynaldo ordered a vodka tonic and Jorge a scotch on the rocks. When the waitress returned with their drinks, she bent over the table as she set the glasses down. Her white blouse must have been at least two sizes too small, her ample breasts looked ready to break out. Jorge could not stop staring, and Reynaldo sniggered.

"It's one hundred Lempiras." She kept a straight face.

He pulled out a hundred Lempira bill and paid her. "Jorge, you pay the next round."

The waitress looked once more at Reynaldo and winked at him before she left.

The lights dimmed a bit, and the boys turned to look at the T-shaped stage below. A woman in a skimpy red two-piece came from behind the black curtains. She danced to the music, moving all around the stage before her finale at the pole. She hugged the pole, then turned around and leaned her back against it, rubbing it sensually up and down.

"Wow, look at that!" Jorge said pointing to the girl. She had turned and now they could see her tanned rounded buttocks. The thread of the G-string was invisible at the distance, giving the impression she was naked.

Reynaldo leaned over the rail of the balcony. He extended his hand, longing to touch the object of his desire. He was desperate to be with a woman for the first time. He craved this one in particular, but he knew she was out of his league, and his price range.

Coming to this club was his consolation prize but also part of the plan. He thought his anxiety to have sex made him nervous when women were around. He figured if he got laid, the anxiety would go and he could appear more confident with his schoolmates. Not that he would brag that he had to pay for sex, but the fact that he knew he had done it would be enough to feel self-assured.

The song ended and the girl was bending over backward from the pole. Reynaldo took the last sip of his vodka.

"Let me order the next round." Jorge signaled the waitress, holding up two fingers.

The waitress arrived with the refill. Jorge pulled out his wallet and paid her.

"What next?" he asked after the girl left.

Reynaldo only shrugged. He did not know how to approach a girl, even if he was planning to pay for the sex.

A new show started on the stage and Jorge stood up, an intense expression on his face. "What the hell. Let's get this going or we will drink all our pussy money."

He left without another word. Reynaldo's heart beat faster. Was this going to be it? Would this be *his* time? He thought he'd die from fright.

Reynaldo watched Jorge talking to the waitress. He looked like he was pleading with her, not negotiating. Reynaldo guessed the price must be high.

He turned to watch the show below. This time, a tall and sure-as-hell fake blonde was dancing to some merengue rhythm. She wore a black baby doll with what looked like velvet covering the appropriate areas, with the rest of her 'costume' sheer chiffon. Her large hoop earrings caught the light, flashing from time to time, along with the broad bracelets on her wrists. She could almost pass for an Amazon. Would she be his Wonder Woman? Jorge's hand on his shoulder broke his train of thought.

"We're all set."

"Really? Who will go, the waitress?"

"Hell, no. If we're paying for it, we better get decent looking ones." Jorge took a large gulp from his glass as he sat down. "We can't do anything here but they let the girls go, for a fee."

"How much?" Reynaldo could not quite believe it.

"Fifteen hundred Lempiras. Plus you pay for the motel and you must either bring them back or send them in a prepaid cab."

"What do you mean *them*?"

"I paid for two," Jorge said.

"What!"

"The waitress saw we were two, so when I asked for one she figured kinky stuff or taking turns or some other porn-fantasy shit. Believe me, it was cheaper to pay for two hookers."

Reynaldo looked down, fifteen hundred Lempiras was more money than he had brought.

"What do you look so gloomy about?"

"I can't afford it. Didn't bring enough. Damn it!"

"Hey, take it easy. Didn't you hear me? I already paid for it."

"But ..."

Jorge held up his hand. "It's not a gift. You owe me, pal."

"How did you pay?"

"I used my father's credit card. He said it was for

emergencies."

"You gave her your credit card?" Jorge must be more desperate than he was.

"No, you moron! I took some money out of an ATM this morning."

"Ah, okay then."

"The waitress was nice though. She's getting us one last round. On the house."

They turned to enjoy the show. Reynaldo wondered who would come with him. Would it be the one in the red thong or the one in the velvet lingerie? His heart raced with anticipation. The wait was over. In just a few minutes, he would go with a woman. He checked his wallet; the condom was in the same place it had been for the past six months. A thought occurred to him, a sudden fright. He checked the expiration date on the wrapping. The condom would be good for another year. He sighed relieved.

Jorge laughed at him. "They give you free ones at the motel in case that one is too old."

"Yeah, I know. But they throw you cheap ones like the ones the government gives away. I prefer to use my own."

"You're so full of shit! If I hadn't known you since we were six, I'd swear you've done this before."

After a few minutes, the waitress arrived with their complimentary drinks. Before leaving, she whispered something into Jorge's ear.

"What did she say?" asked Reynaldo.

"She said she'd go with you for half-price," he said in hushed tone, but could not keep from smiling in mid-sentence.

"Come on! Really, what did she say?"

"She said Sandra and Jasmine will be ready to leave in about twenty minutes. We can enjoy this one," he held his glass up, "without rushing."

"That's nice."

"Three thousand Lempiras will buy you 'nice' anytime."

They toasted and turned to enjoy the show again. When they were done, the waitress returned with two women in tow. Reynaldo stopped breathing – they were the first two dancers they had seen on stage, except now dressed.

The boys stood while the waitress made the introductions before she left. Jasmine, who had worn the red thong, was wearing black jeans, a clinging jersey top with shoestring straps. She also wore cowboy boots. The other dancer, Sandra, had changed into a short, tight denim skirt and loose blouse.

To Reynaldo, they looked even hotter with their clothes on. Jorge took Jasmine's hand. Reynaldo was about to protest, but one look from Jorge reminded him who put out the dough. Jorge had first choice.

The women were about to sit down, but Jorge took a step toward the door. They must have wanted at least a drink or some conversation before getting down to business. How ironic, Reynaldo thought, that even hookers longed for some romance.

Now up close, Reynaldo could see that Sandra's hoop earrings were actually gold. They looked heavy, and pulled down on Sandra's ear lobes. She shrugged and smiled to him as if confirming it was okay to leave without any preamble.

The two couples made their way down the stairs and to the door. The place had packed in more people in the hour since they had arrived. When they exited the building, the women turned and showed navy wristbands to the security guard. Reynaldo figured it was code for 'out on business', or a way to keep tabs on the working girls.

The guard nodded and confirmed Reynaldo's idea by

scribbling something down on a clipboard as he smiled in agreement.

They crossed the street to the spot where they had parked the Nissan. Except now there was a Land Rover parked there instead. Reynaldo and Jorge exchanged glances.

"We parked here, right?" Jorge said.

"I ..." Reynaldo looked up and down the street. It was packed with cars, leaving no more parking available, even for a motorcycle. No Nissan!

"This can't be ..." He shook his head in disbelief, his heart beating fast. An idea formed in his mind; a fearful one, even worse than going into a motel without a condom.

Pulling out his car key, he walked toward the corner. He pressed the alarm button with every step he took, craning his neck in every direction. Hoping to see the twin yellow lights blinking to signal the alarm was off. Cold sweat trickled down his back under his shirt as he returned to where Jorge was.

"So, where's the car?" Sandra said. "I don't like riding a taxi."

CHAPTER TWENTY

DALLAS, TEXAS

Following the directions from a yellow Post-it note, the taxi driver took Sebastian to his dinner appointment. It was in the middle of the suburbs, a good thirty-minute drive from the office. Sebastian wondered how much longer it would be during rush hour. Bill's house looked like a two-family unit and it sat about halfway around the circle at the end of a cul-de-sac. He identified it when he saw his supervisor's set of wheels parked on the curve. Otherwise, the houses were alike. The driver parked the taxi behind Bill's car.

Sebastian paid the cab and walked up the driveway. The sidewalk recently swept judging by the hill of leaves on each side of the house. He wondered, with a pang of guilt, if this had been on his account.

The Knox family owned both of the semi-detached homes, although they lived in the right one. He reached the door. A loveseat swing hung at the far end of the porch.

Not long after Sebastian knocked on the door, Bill opened it. He was clad in his eternal black jeans. The tank top revealed muscular arms usually hidden under a jacket.

"Glad you made it." He held two cans of Budweiser and offered him one.

"Now that *is* a welcome." He traded the bottle of Bordeaux he had brought for the can, and popped it open.

Bill held up the bottle to read the label. "The guy at the store recommended it."

"I'm sure it'll be fine. Come in."

The inside of the house was just as neat as the outside. The living room had twin sofas facing each other, separated by a rectangular coffee table. Sebastian sat while he enjoyed his beer. It was then that he realized his boss had offered him alcohol. He was sure Roger had informed Bill about his drinking problem.

Anyway, he appreciated the fact that Bill had greeted him with the beer. It meant he trusted Sebastian. He vowed to repay this subtle sign of respect by not abusing the trust and set himself a limit of three beers. Would he able to keep his goal? He kept telling everybody he could stop whenever he wanted to. Tonight was a good opportunity to prove it.

Bill's wife came out of the kitchen wearing an apron with a drawing of the map and flag of Texas. Underneath she wore a green short sleeve blouse. The hem of an off-white skirt peeped from behind the apron.

"Hello, Sebastian. I'm glad you could make it. Bill speaks very highly of you." She extended her hand and he shook it.

"Thank you, ma'am."

"Better call me Judy, unless you like the food at your hotel." Her wide smile showed even white teeth.

"I ... er ... I think I prefer to stay, Judy." He smiled.

She turned to Bill, "Dinner will be ready in fifteen minutes. Meantime why don't you show him around?"

"Sure, hon."

Sebastian knew many people who took pride showing off their homes. He had not been like that. In fact, James was the only other person besides his wife and son who had ever walked into his bedroom. He made no comment and prepared for what he thought would be a guided tour of Knox Manor.

Bill stood and led his guest back to the foyer, but instead of taking the stairs, he walked past them and into a door in the back. He opened it and showed Sebastian a home office.

"I don't have to go to the office every day. This computer is connected to the company, so I can download anything I need. Saves lots of time when I'm traveling, if you consider the airport is in the opposite direction from the office."

"The chair looks comfy."

Bill grinned, "Screw you, son."

They went through a corridor to another room. An easel stood in the middle, a canvas with what appeared to be a half-drawn Mona Lisa. Several other canvases showed paintings from other famous artists.

"Painting counterfeits is your retirement plan?"

"Yeah, right. It started as therapy. Damn shrink told me it might help me with the stress. So I took some courses and after a while I loved it. After this, I will do a landscape. Way easier." He grinned.

"The house is bigger than it looks from the outside."

"That's because we're on the other side of the duplex now. Tore down a few walls and Judy has the big kitchen she always wanted and a walk-in closet, too. We converted the living room into an apartment with its own entrance. The rent helps pay the bank."

"Nice plan."

Bill looked at his watch, "We'd better go join Judy"

"Okay."

They headed back to the dining room. Judy had discarded the apron and the aroma of spices he did not recognize filled the room. His own cooking abilities were limited to salads and sandwiches. His stomach rumbled in anticipation. He stopped just to inhale again, to savor it. His mouth watered.

"I reckon you've already heard about my wife's cooking."

He nodded and said, "Also about how exclusive your dinner invitations are!"

"Sebastian, you can sit here." Judy pointed to a chair on the left. Bill took the head of the table and she sat on his right.

He had heard that food is enjoyed first by the nose, then the eyes and last by the tongue. Judy must have known: her food was living proof. She served in the kitchen and brought the individual plates to the table.

Sebastian looked down and admired a twelve-ounce steak, covered with a buttery yellow sauce. He guessed the little black dots sparkling on top were pepper. A perfectly round scoop of mashed potatoes lay on the side. Green beans and carrot sticks completed the feast.

He plucked a carrot stick and was about to pop it into his mouth when he saw the couple had closed their eyes and bowed their heads.

"Dear Lord, we thank thee for the food, the daily job and for all of the little treasures in our life. Amen." Then they ate.

"I didn't know you were the religious type."

"Only about the really important stuff, son."

"The Lord has been good to us," Judy said with visible fervor.

"Yes, I'm sure." He was about to say that God had been so busy looking out for *them* that He had let *his* family die but restrained himself. Instead, he took the last sip from his can.

"Care for another one?" Bill asked.

"No, I'm fine." There was a glass of water next to his plate.

"It's no trouble." Bill stood up and came back from the kitchen with two cans.

"Thank you."

The first bite of the meat convinced Sebastian the

113

black dots were indeed pepper. There were only enough to enhance the taste of the buttery sauce. The meat was so tender it almost melted in his mouth. The vegetables were bathed in olive oil, herbs and spices, al dente and delicious. He preferred not to ruin the sensation with the sour taste of the beer. He did not drink again until after he'd cleared his plate.

All in all, Sebastian felt Judy Knox's reputation was well-deserved. During the meal, she asked about Sebastian's life, about his life growing-up. He entertained them with a few anecdotes of his teenage escapades with James.

"And you still get along with him?" she asked.

"He looks after me a lot."

"That's good. Our two boys were like that, inseparable, but always fighting each other," she commented.

"Poor bastard who ever messed with either of them, pretty soon he'd discover four fists." Bill chuckled.

"Where are they now?"

"Off to college. Both of them on full scholarship."

"Bill! Don't brag about that!"

He shrugged and made no reply. Sebastian had the feeling that it wasn't the first time Bill's comment had been aired. The pride was visible as he took a swig of his beer.

"Is that why you rent some of the space? Too much empty room?" Sebastian took another bite.

"And awfully quiet," she said.

"Yep. Them boys were noisy."

"By the way, Bill tells me you're staying at a hotel."

"Motel," corrected Bill.

Sebastian swallowed before answering. "Yes, it's small but I don't need much space. It seemed convenient as I am still not sure I'll stay here."

"You are doing fine. I told Roger at the meeting. Which brings us to another matter, why don't you check out of that motel and move into the apartment here?"

This took Sebastian off guard. He tried to phrase a gentle refusal. He began to mumble something but Bill held up his hand.

"It's not rent free, son. It is a matter of opportunity. You can't like living out of a suitcase ... we have the place and it is vacant. The way I see it, it's a win-win deal. That what politicians call it."

"I'm not sure."

"Come on, at least think about it." This came from Judy.

That meant she liked the idea too, he thought. Without realizing it, he began counting the pros and cons. The apartment had its own private entrance. He could share a ride with Bill until he got a car. The motel was impersonal at best and the three weeks living there had taken its toll. On the other hand, how would they react if they knew how much he'd been drinking? True he had cut down a bit. He couldn't afford to have people gossip about him going to work with a hangover.

Why did he have to drink in the first place? Oh, yeah. To forget about Kelly and Joshua. Only, he didn't want to forget them. How could he? He drank to forget he no longer had them.

The pain was still there, his heart so crushed it felt like it would choke. The booze eased the pain in his heart, or rather, moved it up to his head. He knew he was bullshitting himself. He felt overwhelmed. He then took the only logical action he could think of: he sipped his beer.

He realized the room had gone quiet. The couple observed him as if they were watching a TV show. Sebastian became self-conscious, embarrassed.

"I'm sorry."

"Never mind. At least you are thinking about it," Judy spoke in a soothing tone.

"Yeah, otherwise going to all this trouble would've been a waste."

"Bill!" She looked shocked but his affable grin made the meaning clear.

"This was your idea of a sales pitch?" Sebastian laughed and they joined him. The tension gone.

"We don't expect you to agree right this minute."

"Okay, I'll think about it. Thanks for the offer. It means a lot."

When Sebastian returned to his motel room that night, he sat on the edge of the bed as he did every night. He poured vodka from the half-empty pint. He held up the glass and got as far as touching the transparent liquor with his lips. They tingled as usual.

Then he put the glass on the table as he realized he did not need to drink that night.

CHAPTER TWENTY ONE

DALLAS, TEXAS

Sebastian stopped typing his report to answer the phone.

"Somebody called from the fire department," Grace said.

"Really? What about?"

"They want you to go check on something. It's about a policy owner. When you get there ask for Paul Mandel."

"Okay." He jotted down the address. He thought he could get there without getting lost.

"And Seb?"

"Yes, Grace."

"They asked for you by name." She cut the connection.

Bill had taken the day off so Sebastian called Roger and explained what Grace had told him. The boss agreed he should go.

He arrived at the address. In the front of an old three-story brick building, two fire engines parked, forming a letter V.

A firefighter dressed in full gear stopped him. Sebastian showed the man his insurance company ID. "Paul Mandel called us."

The man looked at the card, then spoke into his radio. "Paul, a guy named Sebastian Martin is looking for you."

The radio crackled. "Let him pass."

"Negative. The area is not secure for civilians yet."

"Don't worry. The guy is a former FDNY."

Sebastian didn't know his history was common knowledge with the fire department in Dallas. He wondered who this Mandel guy could be. He suspected one of his old chums back in New York had planned a prank on him. Meanwhile, the fireman looked at him in a more appreciative manner.

"That's true?"

Sebastian nodded.

"What the heck you doing now?" The Texas growl was becoming clearer as he spent more time in the Lone Star state.

"Long story." And I really don't want to share it now.

The guy shrugged and let him pass.

The first floor of the building held commercial stores. He peeked inside. Several computer terminals languished in sets of three atop rectangular tables. All the flat screens were blank. He took the corridor in the front center. To his right, a women's clothing store offered fifty percent sales for the coming weekend. He walked the length of the hallway. The smoke had dissipated but the burnt aroma lingered.

At the far end, two unmarked doors remained closed. He guessed one led up and the other down. He made his choice and opened the left one just in time to see another firefighter coming up the stairs. Sebastian took a step back. The man removed the breathing mask to reveal a familiar face.

Sebastian frowned, his mind in overdrive to place a name to the face. The name he didn't remember but before him stood the guy he'd argued with in a bar a few weeks ago.

"Hi, I'm Paul Mandel." He smiled and put out his hand. "Let's put the other day behind us, okay?"

Sebastian shook it. "How do you know I'm from New York?"

"Besides the funny accent you mean?"

"You think New Yorker's have a funny accent?"

"I looked you up," Paul said.

"Checking me out, huh? You gay?"

"Yeah, right. I want a bite out of your big apple!" Paul sneered. "I followed you outside and wrote down the cab's tag."

Sebastian closed his fist. Being sober didn't improve his social skills. Paul seemed to read his mind.

"Listen, we can argue all day or get down to business."

"You called me." Sebastian shrugged. "Lead the way."

Paul led him down a flight of stairs. At the bottom, before opening another door, he handed Sebastian an extra breathing mask, a hardhat and a small flashlight.

"You'll need them inside. When we checked the records, we saw your outfit insures the premises."

He put on the mask, "I was wondering why you had called me. Am I the first one down?"

Paul shook his head. "Arson guy and the police. You're the first civilian though."

"Let's see it."

The firemen pushed the door to the basement. The dark room reeked of smoke.

"You'll notice the construction is old, but has passed previous inspections."

"I'm guessing you didn't call an insurance adjuster just because he bought you a beer, did you?"

"Hell, no!" Paul chuckled.

A few steps inside, Sebastian pointed the light in a grid pattern, trying to see the real reason he had been summoned.

Four rooms, divided by wood paneling, comprised the basement. They crossed to a door into a small room.

119

Four queen-size mattresses lay on the floor, one in each corner of the room.

"People live here?"

"The beds give you that idea?" Paul's tone embraced a heavy dose of sarcasm.

That was the problem with alpha-male environments, thought Sebastian. The fire department in New York was an alpha-male environment and the same macho stance applied to Dallas. Sebastian had to prove he was worth his salt.

Sebastian considered Paul's reply for a moment. Paul wanted to show him something, but Sebastian had to figure it out by himself.

He pointed the light upward. The low ceiling had no paneling. He could see the plumbing between this room and the floor above, as well as the sprinkler system. The flashlight highlighted something. A plastic bag filled with liquid. He moved the light to reveal several more hanging bags, connected with a thin rope.

"Are those bags what I think they are?"

"Only if you think they're filled with gasoline."

"Holy shit!"

Paul held up a clear plastic evidence bag. "This is the primer. The guy must be old-school. He placed a candle on a gas-filled plate in the center of the room. When the flame caught, the mattresses started to burn."

"Hmmm, mattresses don't usually give you flame, just smoke."

"I guess he didn't know that. That piece of trivia saved the place. They made lots of smoke, enough to go up."

"The clothing store?"

"Yep, they called us."

"What happened with the sprinklers?"

"Disabled."

Sebastian took a closer look at the wall panels attached

to several columns, which supported the weight of the building. He approached the wall. Something looked odd, but he could not put his finger on it. He frowned. The spotlight swept up and down the column, and then he stopped at something else about mid-height.

He stared at it, concentrated. What was wrong with this picture? He willed the columns to answer, but they didn't obey, just stared back at him.

"You want to move them with your mind?"

Smiling he shook his head. "Something's wrong with that column but I can't figure out what."

"Maybe it is the lousy finishing. There's about an inch missing at the bottom. If it weren't for the smoke, I bet you'd see around the entire room." Eager to prove his point, Paul approached and placed his gloved finger in the gap, then turned his head in Sebastian's direction.

"Maybe." Sebastian wasn't convinced yet.

A soft rumble, similar to an earthquake, came from above.

"What the hell?" Paul said.

Then Sebastian got it. He knew what the owner had done – the bastard had weakened the columns.

"We need to go," he urged Paul.

When Paul turned to leave, the rumble grew louder, then grew to ear-shattering proportions. Something grazed his arm.

Sebastian looked up. Lines that resembled lightning bolts appeared across the floor above and chunks of plaster fell down. Sebastian and Paul rushed to the exit as the pieces raining on them grew in size. Sebastian inwardly thanked Paul for his hardhat.

They reached the door but before they got out, the floor above collapsed on them amidst a thunderous cloud of rubble, dust and the remains of the fire smoke. Some of the plastic bags burst and created isolated small fires that filled the room with black smoke.

Sebastian lay face down on the floor; his hands over his head. The room went quiet as the last pieces of debris dropped down.

He moved his arms. They hurt, felt bruised, but functioning. He tried his legs. That proved more difficult. He looked down through the settling dust. A large piece of cement covered him from the waist down, like a short and heavy sheet. He pushed and heaved, but accomplished nothing. He saw his shoes on the far end. He craned his neck, squinted his eyes. A dark shape – he guessed it was Paul – lay just a few feet to his right, by the door.

He wondered about the people outside. They'd vacated the building, he felt certain. The Fire Department personnel had to wait, to hold off until the dust settled before they could go into the building.

In the meantime, he had to stay calm. What else could he do? His gaze roamed around the room until he focused on the dark shadow that was Paul Mandel. All air tanks worn by the department made a sound, a low hiss, signifying an officer was down. He was familiar with the sound. He had heard an ominous concerto of them, coming from all his fallen colleagues on 9/11. The hiss that had brought him many nightmares sounded loud and clear now. Paul needed help. There was little he could do while pinned to the ground.

No doubt about his first priority: get free. He heaved up; all his might failed to move the cement blanket even an inch.

He let go and sighed. Perhaps he could slide out, like the snake that bit Jill. Using his hands for leverage, he pushed and wiggled his body. That worked better. He bent his knees shortening the length under the cement sheet. Sweat trickled down his face. Sebastian puffed and heaved until his legs came out.

He thought it better not to stand, and crawled to

where Paul lay. He shook him; no response. He felt for a pulse and found a strong, steady beat; Paul's chest moved up and down. Sebastian would have sworn the man was asleep if it wasn't for the pile of rubble covering him.

The sound of broken glass, then a sudden shout came from above. "Paul, are you there?"

Sebastian looked up, and without the ceiling in the way, he could see a window. Another firefighter in full gear stood outside leaning through the broken glass.

"He's unconscious, but I think he's okay. Get us out of here."

"Working on it." The man disappeared.

He assessed the room with a trained eye. The stairs were at the far end of the room, so it was not an option to go through there. He looked up again. Dust particles glittered against the sunlight filtering down. So close and yet so far away.

The man returned, this time accompanied, and with a short ladder. Sometimes the easiest solutions were the best. The firefighters placed the ladder through the nonexistent ceiling, resting the plastic tips on the uneven ground.

"We'll hold it tight. Can you climb up?"

In response, Sebastian stood up.

"You're okay. Come on up."

Sebastian shook his head. "Not yet."

"Come on, don't waste any time. You need to get out," the man barked.

Sebastian looked down, used his boot to clear the bigger chunks of rubble covering Paul. He spread his feet apart for better support and hoisted him up, puffed and grunted, then swung Paul over his shoulder. "Damn it, Paul. You're heavy!"

The few steps to cross the room to reach the ladder were like walking over a minefield. With each step, he made sure he had secure footing before shifting his weight. Smaller pieces of rubble gave under his weight. A big one almost made him trip, but he managed to reach the ladder with his free hand.

With renewed stability, he took some air, and to the astonishment of the two men above, he climbed one rung at a time. Slow but steady, shifting his weight to each leg until he reached the top. The men at the top took care of their partner.

Sebastian walked out to the street. The yellow tape prevented curious onlookers from getting too close. He turned to the building. As soon as the two firefighters carrying Paul stepped off the sidewalk, there was a rumble and a thunderous noise. The ground shook and the entire three-floor building collapsed into itself.

He felt drawn back in time to lower Manhattan, to the same anguish, the same smell of dust. His heart beat faster and he closed his eyes. The sound of the countless beeps, replaced by Kelly's screams as she flew out the plane. His conscious knew he could not hear Kelly, but the piercing sound of her shrieks filled his ears. Even now. Every time.

He ran to escape the falling debris, a dust cloud enveloping him and everything within reach, as everything darkened. He kept running until he reached the back of an ambulance.

He opened the back door. The three firefighters appeared beside him. The four men climbed into the vehicle and closed the doors behind them. Inside, Paul had come round, coughing into the air mask. His eyes closed, one hand gripped the rail of the gurney, the knuckles white.

Then silence. Complete. Ominous. No other sound but Paul's heavy breathing. They stepped out. The site where a three-story brick building used to be was now a pile of rubble, glass, and dust.

"Nobody inside?" Sebastian wanted to make sure.

"Nope. We evacuated as soon as we came," said one of the other firefighters.

Sebastian breathed out, relieved.

"They told me you carried me up." Paul said.

Sebastian flashed him a cocky smile, "Yes. Now you owe me a beer *and* your life."

Paul remained serious, looked straight at Sebastian, and held out his hand.

Sebastian shook it, knowing full well what it meant. A thank you, and a friend for life.

"Dude, it's official. You're his bitch now." The other man said and the four men laughed.

Other firefighters started to mill about. One shouted orders to control the crowd; others ran the lines, all following instructions for such a crisis.

Sebastian watched as the operation ran with smooth efficiency. There was nothing he would have done differently. He knew all the procedures, yet he no longer belonged to the Fire Department. Sheer luck had him there smack in the middle of it.

"The D.A. is going to have his hands full. I think he'll go after the owner." Sebastian said.

Paul nodded. "Arson is going to be the least of his offences now. With any luck, the D.A. will push for attempted murder."

"Considering all the people who were supposed to be at work inside, I can see them building a solid case."

"Poor bastard will wish he'd been inside."

CHAPTER TWENTY TWO

DALLAS, TEXAS

Sebastian met Bill and Roger in the latter's office, and together they went over several cases.

Roger had a keen mind and probed the conclusions his investigators presented him. Take nothing for granted seemed to be his motto.

On one particular case, because the conclusion was inconclusive, Roger probed deeper. He picked up his phone and asked Grace to get a hold of somebody. Sebastian did not hear the name. It sounded Latino but he could not be certain.

When Grace transferred the call, Roger put it on speakerphone. This time, Sebastian got the name, Gustavo Fonseca, of Honduras. The speakerphone generated a weird metallic ring in Gustavo's voice.

Roger informed Gustavo that Bill and Sebastian were also in his office, and then went straight to business. "There is a four year gap," he summed up.

"I've seen similar cases before. My bet is that the boy never existed." Bill paused then thought of another possibility, "Or the dead one wasn't covered on the policy."

"Gustavo, have you met with the coroner?" asked Roger.

"Yes."

"And?" Roger prompted.

"I don't know him enough to trust him. His reaction

looked genuine." Gustavo had a heavy accent, but his English was good.

"Anyone can be an actor," protested Bill.

"Movies are not a booming industry in Honduras, Bill." Gustavo protested.

"Oh, come on! You have politicians, don't you?"

"Yes, but—"

"Then you do have great liars south of the border, just as we have them here!" he declared, earning a collective chuckle on both ends of the connection.

All through the exchange, Sebastian had remained quiet, wondering if he'd ever be as cynical.

"Given all the paperwork, you're saying the death certificate is the only thing you would take as real, correct?"

"Yes, Mr. Simmons." Gustavo's tone carried conviction.

"I guess we can spare the doctor this time, huh?"

That comment got Sebastian's attention. "What?"

"Ancient history," said Bill in a dismissive manner.

"Five years is not old enough," countered Roger.

Sebastian felt like the sober guy who had just run into his drunken friends to hear the punch line of the joke. He felt out of place. The three men had a history together, and they knew all the jokes. He despised being the rookie after years of being at the top. He wondered if his decision to be here was the correct one.

"Sebastian," Roger brought him back, "like I was saying, five years ago a guy took out a policy with us. He was dead within a week."

"And of course, something other than a rotten corpse started to smell," interjected Bill.

"Literally," commented Roger. Then he added, "This happened on Gustavo's turf. The policy was for a little over a million dollars, so I decided to send Bill to lend a hand as well.

"They interviewed everybody and I mean that in the strictest terms. Wife, kids, business associates, college

127

girlfriends. When the smell was evident but the proofs lacking, we got an order to exhume the body."

Intrigued, Sebastian said, "What happened then?"

"When we dug up the coffin, we found two sacks of first grade cement." Roger said.

"That sounds like something to write a novel about," Sebastian commented.

"I heard it's in the works by a local author," crackled the speaker.

Sebastian digested the information. He visualized the opening of the coffin and imagined the surprise at what they found inside. Although he knew Honduras was considered a third-world country, he could not believe it would be that easy to pull a stunt like that, by just one person alone. He went over it in his mind step by step: if they had to exhume it, it meant it had to be buried. Duh! But that also meant a possible wake, some kind of religious service. He remembered attending services with closed coffins because of the injuries, the victim burned in fires, for example. But still, the body had to be prepped. The body. That sent his mind in another direction.

"A doctor signed a death certificate, right?" he deduced.

"Told you his nose was in the right place," Bill said with a tinge of pride in his voice.

"Yes," responded Roger. "The doctor was the weakest link in that chain. We went after him, with everything we had. He confessed to receiving a bonus to issue the certificate without seeing the corpse. He lost his license to practice medicine."

"Damn bastard had to find another way to make a living."

"So, in this case, you think the doctor was not involved, is that it?" Sebastian summed it up.

"Correct."

Roger shared a look with Bill who nodded in agreement. "Gustavo, we'll call you right back, okay?"

"*No hay problema.*"

After killing the connection, Roger's expression turned serious. He sat up straight.

"Sebastian, we've reached crunch time. This case is the perfect example of the travel that is required." He paused. "Now, Bill here has to make the trip, but it is not fair to him to send him abroad all the time, even more so when we have two investigators in-house."

While considering this development, Sebastian looked straight into Roger's eyes. He could tell the man was resolved. Sebastian understood what was required of him.

"I see," he said, to gain time before giving his answer.

"I won't lie. We are very satisfied with your performance. Bill has said, and more than once," he shot a side-glance at Bill, "that you have good instincts. However, I have the same concerns as the first time you walked through that door," he pointed past behind Sebastian. "Now, can you or can you not do the required travel?"

Sebastian took his time before responding. He felt the men with him deserved a proper explanation for his actions.

Measuring his words, he said, "I have not stepped into an airplane since the day my family died." He held up a hand when Roger tried to say something. "Please, let me finish. It is not a fear of heights or that I dread having an accident as they did. I do not like to travel that way because of what I lost. I appreciate the opportunity you have given me."

He had made a decision and now was time to live up to it. "When I shook your hand back in the hospital, I said I'd do the job. I stand by my word."

CHAPTER TWENTY THREE

DALLAS, TEXAS

"We are now boarding passengers seated rows sixteen to six. Passengers seated rows sixteen to six, please stand in line to board now."

This was the moment Sebastian dreaded the most. He took a deep breath, stood up, and wheeled his bag. He stood in line behind a businesswoman. Her jacket and skirt suit were a dark shade of pink, pink shoes and even a matching suitcase. At least she was not blonde, he thought.

When it was his turn, he presented his boarding pass. The same young guy who had made the announcement on the PA took a cursory look at the pass and waved him inside the sleeve corridor.

He walked the length of the sleeve but stopped in front of the plane door. The last time he had crossed a similar threshold, he walked in a happy man but jumped out a widower and a bereaved father.

A female flight attendant in a tight uniform greeted every one with a frozen smile. She looked ominous, her makeup lurid under the plane's bright white light.

He closed his eyes and the faces of Joshua and Kelly appeared before him. He tried to concentrate on a happy memory. Just like Peter Pan, he needed a happy thought to take off.

The happy memory never came. Instead, he felt the bump as another passenger tried to pass him. Opening his eyes, he caught the flight attendant staring at him. Afraid she'd think he might be a terrorist, he moved along.

He could not help thinking that before 9/11, his attitude would have only warranted an annoyed look, afraid of a needy, attention-seeking passenger but nothing more. Holding his bag tight, he took the final step onto the cabin, lifting the case over the entry way.

"Good evening. Do you know your seat number?" The business-like smile appeared again.

"Seven C."

"Seventh row. Aisle seat on your right."

Sebastian walked past the first five rows of leather seats in first class. Some indistinct elevator music filled the air. He reached his row, placed the bag in the overhead bin, and sat down.

Seats A and B were already occupied by a mother and son. The boy could not have been much older than Joshua would have been now. He mused about whether God had a warped sense of humor; maybe the creator was just cynical.

Okay, he thought, at least the woman looked very different from Kelly; long wavy black hair and brown eyes and not short fair hair and blue eyes.

He buckled up and leaned back; he thought that the little crisis at the door might have been reported to the undercover U.S. Marshal, so he would keep an eye on Sebastian during the flight. Then again, maybe because the Marshal was supposed to be undercover, the flight attendant may not know who he was. Anyway, he felt sure the incident was logged somewhere. Traveling had become very complicated, damn it.

The first half hour of the flight was pretty uneventful. Chewing gum reduced the humming in his ear to a manageable level. The flight attendants were busy serving the passengers. The stale air smelled like antiseptic nothingness. The woman had switched seats with her son, who remained glued to the small window.

Sebastian looked around and everybody seemed immersed in his or her own private universe. A man in his early twenties was air drumming to the beat from his iPod. Only God knew if he was in time.

Next to him sat a businesswoman, typing on her laptop with enough force that Sebastian predicted the need for a replacement inside of two months. Another woman wearing headphones occupied the window seat, nodding to the muted sound only she could hear.

Each of them confined inside their own little bubble, Sebastian thought. He checked his watch, another hour and fifty minutes to go.

Closing his eyes, the face of his dead son appeared. This time his son's eyes were wide open with fear. Sebastian opened his eyes, looked down, and saw his right arm holding the armrest in a white-knuckle grip. He willed his hand to let go; it took all his might to calm his galloping heart. Sweat broke out on his forehead. He could feel the cold drops trickling down the side of his face.

He remembered the day before, when he'd spoken to Doctor Jones who had suggested a pill, a mild sedative, for this trip. He had warned Sebastian about the possibility of an anxiety attack. Adopting a macho stance, he dismissed the doctor, claiming only women suffered from nervous attacks.

Was that what was happening to him? He felt emasculated. When was the last time he had been with a woman? It was not the sex he missed, but in that moment, he despaired of being able to prove himself a man. Suddenly the humming faded out, and he heard his own breathing instead. He was hyperventilating.

He had to man up. What to do? How should he cope with his fears? Then again, a man is not supposed to have fears, or at least not show any! Men as the source of strength, the pillar for a family to rely on … all that crap was an outdated concept. Still, walking into buildings on fire did not scare him as much as living in misery the rest of his life.

132

"Would you like to something to drink?" The female voice brought him into focus. She represented the lifeline he was in desperate need of, now that it was too late to get the pill.

He uttered his order in a single monotone sentence. The attendant must have sensed something amiss. She did not even ask the other two people on the row and poured the clear liquid into a plastic cup, then added a measure of orange juice.

Sebastian took the cup with the eagerness of a baby awaiting his bottle. He emptied the sweet-sour drink in two gulps. By the time the attendant had finished serving the woman and son, Sebastian raised his hand rattling the ice cubes against the cup. The attendant hesitated for a second, but served him another one.

This time Sebastian sipped from it. The alcohol had not yet reached his head, but knowing it would get there gave him a sense of peace. He knew it was a twisted form of comfort, but he was grateful for the means to endure the flight.

* * * *

SAN PEDRO SULA, HONDURAS

Gustavo arrived at the San Pedro Sula airport early. He parked his car and walked toward terminal A. His sunglasses turned everything to shades of yellow, enhancing details, but even so, he did not see the speeding vehicle that almost ran over him. At the last instant, Gustavo jumped back.

The car did not even slow down, but the window rolled down and an arm stuck out giving him the finger. From instinct, Gustavo reached for his gun. His hand wrapped around the Lexan grip of his A.S.P. He stopped short of pulling out the pistol.

"Control," he said aloud. "You must control yourself. He's not out to kill you. He is just an average jerk behind a wheel."

Standing on the edge of the street that separated the parking lot from the terminal, he released his grip and counted to ten. This time, he looked both ways before crossing.

The Ramon Villeda Morales International Airport was small in comparison with others he had visited abroad. The building was less than twenty years old. During Hurricane Mitch, which had hammered the country in 1998, the building had flooded – to the roof. A few months afterwards, when Gustavo had taken a trip, he'd seen the marks on the inside of the building showing the high level it had reached. He'd been shocked. Fresh paint now covered the stains, but the places where they had been were burned into his memory and he could see them, or rather feel they were there, beneath the coat of paint.

The automatic doors slid open. He felt the rush of air coming down from above the door. His tennis shoes made squeaky sounds on the polished marble floor. The ceiling was very high, almost three floors. People milled around in the usual airport buzz: hugs or kisses for goodbye or welcome.

He wondered about Sebastian Martin. Bill Knox said he was a good man, sharp and also very tall. At five-nine, Gustavo stood a tad above the average Honduran. However, he expected Sebastian to be well over six feet.

He approached the International Arrivals area and waited just outside a set of automatic sliding doors that would only open from the inside. About two dozen people hung out by the door waiting for travelers.

He caught a couple holding cards with names written on them. He hated those cards, both using them when meeting somebody and arriving somewhere to see his name out in the open like that. Somehow, he felt exposed.

The doors opened, and a man walked out. He wore a black linen shirt with a heavy gold chain hung around his neck. Two girls of about ten-years-old rushed to embrace him. More people came out, and the joy of families coming together was contagious. Gustavo found himself smiling at a happy couple who greeted each other with a long, hard kiss.

Then he spotted a walking tower, and guessed he must be Sebastian. He wore faded baggy jeans, a plaid shirt, worn loose, that could not hide the early stages of a potbelly, and brown Caterpillar boots.

The man looked like a lumberjack. The strong forearms showed the truth about his past good shape. The way he walked had something unusual about it, a sway to it. He seemed dizzy. Gustavo knew about the loss of his family and the hard time he was going through. He decided not to mention any of this. Better to stick to business. He approached him and extended his hand.

"Sebastian Martin?"

The man turned his head in Gustavo's direction, his eyes looked overly tired, and his handshake was limp.

"So you are our man in Honduras," Sebastian said.

"Guess so." Somebody had more than one little drink on the plane.

They walked back to his car. The bright orange caught the gringo's eye. "What kind of car is that?"

"It's a Lada Niva. Made in the Soviet Union."

"It looks robust. Never rode in a commie car before."

"They were popular in the early eighties. My father bought this one new from the dealer. I bought it from him a few years ago."

Opening the back hatch, Gustavo let Sebastian put in his single bag and closed the door. They got in, and Gustavo put the key in the ignition.

Sebastian raised an eyebrow. "The switch is on the left side?"

Gustavo nodded. "Most of the things on this car are left-side oriented. You know, coming from a left-wing country."

"Really?"

"Try to roll down the window."

Sebastian tried to move the handle to the left; it did not budge. He smiled and tried the opposite direction. At once, the window eased down.

"What about the windshield wiper?"

"Opposite, too. They move from left to right." Using his right arm, he imitated the horizontal position of the wiper, then moved it ninety degrees to reach full vertical. He repeated the motion a couple of times.

"Maybe it was more a political statement because I don't think there are lots of left-handed people in the Soviet Union." Gustavo explained. "And, of course, they drive on the wrong side of the road!"

Gustavo turned the key and the engine caught on the first attempt. He was proud of his well-maintained car. The engine sounded heavy, powerful.

"Like I said, robust," Sebastian said signaling with his head toward the front.

"It's only four cylinders."

"No way!"

"I'm not lying."

Sebastian whistled, impressed. He looked around the interior. The seats were black synthetic leather wannabe; the dashboard was simple, as a plain utility vehicle should be, with two round vents in the center.

"Because of the weather there, this baby came with heat, not air conditioning."

Sebastian's face, already flushed from the hot, humid Caribbean weather, went redder. His eyebrows arched up in obvious anguish.

"But I installed one." Gustavo said as he turned a knob in the center of the dashboard. Sebastian's sigh was one of obvious relief.

Hot air rushed out at first, but cold air soon circulated. It took a couple of minutes for the unit to blow enough to make a perceptible change in the interior.

"Where are we going?"

"Downtown. You're staying at the Hotel Sula."

"Is it good?"

"Yes. It is right at the heart of town, across from the central park. The cathedral and the city hall are also facing the park. That's where the grand hotels used to be."

Driving out of the parking lot, Gustavo entered the four-lane boulevard that led to the main road. A World War II airplane rose on a cement pedestal. Gunmetal gray, the cockpit closed, the fighter tilted down slightly, in attack position. A monument to the past glories of aviation.

"Why is that there?"

"It's the entrance to the Air Force base."

"Really. How good is your air force?"

"Very." Gustavo added, "They're rated the best in Central America. We have a school that is very popular. Heck, it's run by gringos."

"Didn't know that."

"Oh yes, very big. Established back in the eighties, when we were a bastion for democracy. We share a border with Nicaragua down South, so President Reagan made sure the Red Aggression didn't move any farther North."

"Interesting."

A bypass connected them to a parkway where traffic was heavier. Gustavo stayed on that road until it continued into the main street. The street was narrower, and cars traveled both ways.

"This is the original San Pedro Sula city limit. We are approaching the central park, just a few more blocks up ahead."

A traffic light on almost every corner made for a very slow pace. Gustavo could see his guest was anxious and uncomfortable. For sure, he was too big for this car. There was no faster way to reach the hotel. He stopped at yet another light.

Sebastian whistled. Gustavo followed his line of sight and

137

saw he was impressed with the building that rose on their left.

"How old is that cathedral?"

"Not even a hundred years. Construction began in the late forties, using classic Spanish colonial design."

"No wonder it looks older. Where's the hotel? You said it was somewhere around here?"

"That building on the corner is a bank." Gustavo pointed to his right, across the street. "The hotel is right next to it."

When the light turned, Gustavo advanced half a block and stopped outside the hotel. A bellhop approached the car.

"I can't park here. You can go with him while I leave the car around the corner."

"Sure."

* * * *

Twenty minutes later, they were in Sebastian's room on the eighth floor. The décor was simple but efficient. Two queen beds took most of the walking space. On the opposite side, a sliding double door led to a small balcony overlooking the city. They sat outside on the balcony, drinking Scotch on the rocks from a small bottle Gustavo had brought with him.

"Lots of large buildings. I think I saw every U.S. franchise we have back home. If it weren't for the Spanish on the signs I wouldn't know I had left America."

"Hey, I've been to New York. This looks nothing like it."

"Well, not New York or any major city, but it could pass for a small town. Does everyone here speak English? I mean, you speak it well."

Gustavo laughed at that. "You could say that. We know English is the business language of the world, so everybody tries to learn. Gringos bring the money." He paused for a minute; he had to get something out of the way. "I heard what happened to you. I don't know the details but I'm sorry about your family."

"Thank you. Still think of them every day."

Gustavo thought it best to change the topic. "Bill told me you were a fireman." Sebastian nodded. "What rank?"

"Lieutenant. Technically, I am still on leave. Not sure if they'll downgrade me when I retire."

"I don't think they will. I was also a lieutenant. But in the army, Special Forces."

"Cool. Funny how same rank serves for fighting wars and for saving lives."

"I didn't peg you for a tree-hugger," said Gustavo.

"No, I'm not. Just never been a fan of wars, or guns for that matter. How about you?"

"Hell, yes. I'd establish a local branch of the NRA if they'd let me."

"I thought you walked funny. Gun on the ankle?"

"No." Gustavo said with a smile. "Small of the back." He pulled out his handgun and held it up.

Sebastian leaned forward for a better look at the pistol. He frowned.

"Why do I see the bullets?"

"The stocks are made of clear Lexan. In a combat situation you don't count bullets, this way you can tell your ammo at a glance."

"You thought of that?"

"I wish. No, this gun is an A.S.P. made by Theodore Paris, an armorer in New York. He developed it for your secret service."

"So it can kill better."

"In a word, yes. This guy Paris took apart a Smith & Wesson and made a bunch of improvements. Sights, the Lexan grips, all designed for a faster retrieve and shoot."

"Army men and their guns," Sebastian mused. He gulped the last of the liquor remaining in the glass. "Let's get a refill." Sebastian grabbed Gustavo's glass and went inside.

Alone for a moment, Gustavo weighed his conversation so far with the big Sebastian Martin. He seemed a decent fellow. Bill warned him about Sebastian's drinking, but he figured after losing a family, he would want to drink himself to death too.

Although sympathetic, he was careful not to show it. He knew how irritated people could be when thought they were being pitied. He'd brought the bottle of scotch knowing full well what he was doing.

He checked his watch. They'd been talking for almost an hour and a half, and this was the third drink. Gustavo had thought that Sebastian would drain it in a rush but was now amazed at how slowly he drank. He decided to give Sebastian a good welcome and he fished his cell phone out of his pocket to make the call.

* * * *

Sebastian poured the scotch. The buzz from the vodka on the plane had died down.

He liked this Gustavo fellow so far. The man talked too much, put too much stock in his possessions, but was okay overall.

"So, about this case of yours. Where do we stand?" Sebastian said as he returned and handed a glass back to Gustavo.

"The boy died by drowning in Puerto Cortes. The paperwork says he was supposed to be eight, but he really looked more like twelve."

"You visited the hospital?"

"Yes, like I said in our conference call. I have to say I believe the doctor."

"Maybe there were two different kids, so can't be certain. What of the parents?"

"Saved them for last. I preferred to gather all the info so I can ask the right questions."

"Can we go there tomorrow?"

"Sure."

Sebastian then asked about Gustavo's family. Bummer he was divorced, but seemed to be coping well with it. A knock on the door surprised Sebastian.

140

"Did you order room service?"

Gustavo looked dubious, "That's one way to describe it," he said with a mischievous grin.

The Honduran went to open the door. Two women came in. One, mid-twenties maybe, wore faded jeans, a knit top. The high-heels were a shocking red, but worst of all, they almost matched her hair color. The other one was dark haired, more formal in a skirt and blouse. Gustavo greeted them both with a kiss on the cheek.

Sebastian stiffened. Surely Gustavo had not just invited hookers into his room? The women walked in, past Gustavo, who closed the door. His fear was confirmed when he saw the casual way Gustavo caressed the backside of the one wearing the skirt.

"What are you doing?"

"I figured you'd had no action for a while. That thing might fall off, you know."

"When did you arrange this?" He feared the idea might go all the way back to Dallas.

"Spur of the moment. Honest. I called them when you served the last round."

Sebastian felt the color return to his face. "Listen, I—"

"Come on," Gustavo interrupted him, then leaned closer and whispered in his ear, "this time is on me."

He would not be lured into this. "I'm not interested."

"Don't be so rude to them. Here, let me introduce you. Tricky, because they don't speak English." He smiled. "But you won't be talking much anyway, right?"

Sebastian was furious. He had been faithful to Kelly. After her death, he had remained celibate. The feelings for his wife ran so deep he still felt married. Had he said something to Gustavo that made him think he needed or wanted to get laid?

He didn't care, he didn't want to. They had to leave.

"This is Gloria," Gustavo stroked the bare shoulder. "She works in a *maquila* during the day."

141

Does she go to work with that hair? Sebastian wondered. Then he figured it must be a wig. They might not understand English, but they certainly would understand universal body language. Before Gustavo could introduce the other one, he stepped between them. He went and opened the door and stood with his thumb signaling outside.

"What's wrong?"

"Listen to me." Experience had taught him how intimidating his deep voice could be, and he used it to the full now. "I do not want to sleep with any woman. Paid or otherwise." He paused for effect. "I am mourning my wife and if you don't understand that, then at least, respect it."

The women seemed to understand; they looked at the door, then at Sebastian, and last at Gustavo who nodded. They left without saying a word.

Sebastian did not close the door. He looked at Gustavo who asked, "Me too?"

"Yes!"

"This is what I get for trying to help?"

"Here's a tip. Next time, find out what a person needs before you provide."

"I got the Scotch right."

"Booze is one thing. Hell, I drank while she was alive! Now, get out."

Gustavo sighed, looked at the carpet, as if searching for something else to say. After a second, he took a step toward the door. Once outside, he turned to face Sebastian. "We still have to work together."

"I'll see you here at nine," Sebastian said before he slammed the door shut.

CHAPTER TWENTY FOUR

Sebastian Martin did not wait outside the hotel. It was nine o'clock but felt like noon under the brilliant sun. Nights were not so bad, but the heat during the day was more than his New York attitude could handle. And the humidity! Okay, New York did get hot during the summer, but never like this. A few minutes outside and his shirt was stuck to his back. He felt so dirty he ran back upstairs to change, as he considered changing his views on global warming too. This time he paced the marble floor of the lobby. He could see through the door and step out the minute that orange contraption of a car pulled up.

After Gustavo left the previous evening, Sebastian placed a call through the hotel to Bill Knox to check in. He told the Texan his opinion of Gustavo Fonseca in general and decided to let the stunt with the hookers slide.

"It looks like everything he owns has to have a meaning, a back story. His gun was made for the Secret Service, the car is Russian made and belonged to his father."

"I remember the Niva. He was reluctant to install the aircon. I had to tell him I'd hire somebody else in the country if he didn't!"

Bill prepped Sebastian on how to handle himself during the day's interview with the parents of the dead boy. There was a chance they might not speak English, but his job was to study the body language, look at how the father interacted with the mother. Sebastian wouldn't need Spanish for that.

He saw the Lada slide into view and he walked toward it. Gustavo leaned over to unlock the door, and Sebastian climbed in.

"How are you this morning?"

"Fine, but I'm sweating like a pig."

"You'll get used to it in a couple of days."

"Hope so. Bill says hello by the way."

Gustavo put the car into gear and drove off. Sebastian observed he did not turn but kept going along the same street. A few blocks away he saw a rather large construction to the right.

"That's the old soccer stadium with a capacity for twenty-five thousand enthusiasts. The new larger one can hold almost double. It's by the airport," said Gustavo.

"I missed it last night."

"Different street. We didn't drive by it."

The Honduran turned right into an ample, clean avenue. At the end of the block, adjacent to the stadium, Sebastian pointed to something familiar.

"That's the original fire station."

"Those look like really old fire engines," Sebastian said.

Gustavo shrugged. "I guess so. Firemen are very dedicated but you know people, they don't care about the department until their houses need saving."

"Shame."

"I know."

Sebastian made a note to call some of his old buddies in the department. There must be something they could get for their Honduran counterparts.

Two blocks on, Gustavo made a left turn and parked about halfway down the block.

"This is Barrio Los Andes. Used to be upper middle

class but people have moved to the suburbs and this area has become more commercial. Fewer people live here every year."

Sebastian looked around; he spotted a flower shop, a video store, a security firm, and a large green house. He followed Gustavo to the house in the middle and watched as he pressed the doorbell.

A woman craned her neck over the low fence. She spoke in Spanish. Gustavo replied and Sebastian guessed he was giving their details and reason for the visit. She frowned, added something else, and went back inside.

"She's the maid," explained Gustavo. "She went back to see if Mister Delgado could receive us."

"A maid? They must be well off."

"You'd think so, but no. Labor is cheap in this country. Most people used to have maids, usually girls from the countryside. Now, with the garment factories that have spread around the city, they have become scarce but not unheard of."

The maid returned, and this time she opened the fence and led them to a living room. Two large wicker sofas formed an L-shape against the walls. A coffee table stood in the center, also wicker but with a glass top. Sebastian estimated the room to be at least twenty feet wide by fifty feet long. A tall cabinet doubled as a partition to define the space for the dining table at the far end and the living room, where they'd entered.

The maid signaled them to sit down then disappeared through a door in the center of the room. Sebastian walked toward the cabinet and looked at several framed pictures displayed there; most showed parties, people celebrating. The same couple appeared on almost every one, and so did a little boy. In one, the boy was blowing out candles on a cake while surrounded by smiling faces.

Gustavo sat down on the sofa facing the length of the room; after a minute Sebastian followed suit and sat

145

beside him.

Soon after, a man came from the far end. He looked to be in his mid-forties, dark skinned, black curly hair, speckled with white on the sides. He had two days' worth of stubble on his cheeks. He wore a short sleeve shirt over faded blue jeans and leather sandals.

He exchanged a few words with Gustavo that seemed to be introductions, for Gustavo put out his hand. The man shook it. Sebastian felt weird with nothing to do, so he fashioned a polite smile and shook the man's hand. His handshake was firm, his hands calloused, used to manual labor.

"Hello," the man said. He had a thick accent. "I'm Miguel Delgado. Please sit down. My wife is coming soon."

They sat and the man joined them. The maid returned with two glasses of water on a tray. She put the tray on the coffee table and disappeared into the kitchen again.

Sebastian stole a glance at Gustavo, who picked up his water. The room filled with an awkward silence. A plump woman came from the same door as Mr. Delgado. Gustavo and Sebastian rose to meet her. Mr. Delgado remained seated but said something to her that sounded like a barked order. Gustavo made the introductions. Sebastian shook hands with her. Her hand was cold. She sat by her husband.

Gustavo spoke a few words to them, and they nodded. He stopped and turned toward Sebastian.

"He speaks little English and she doesn't at all. Is there any question you want me to relay to them?"

"No. Just what we discussed yesterday. You go ahead and fill me in later."

Gustavo nodded and rattled on in a monologue, explaining what they were concerned about. Sebastian saw how the woman rubbed her husband's leg, her head

146

tilted to one side, listening to Gustavo. At certain points, she made almost imperceptible nods. Mr. Delgado kept a straight face, his eyes locked on the speaker, his hands set firmly on his knees.

Sebastian leaned forward to grab his glass of water. He studied the couple's legs. Her tapping right leg betrayed her nervousness. The man's feet were still but at an odd, wide angle. Sebastian did his best to keep from frowning and sipped from his glass.

Gustavo finished speaking and looked straight at Mrs. Delgado. She fidgeted, turned to look at her husband, and mumbled a quiet reply. The man leaned forward and placed a restraining hand on her leg. He spoke with confidence but his tone was somewhat evasive, his sentences short and blunt. Gustavo asked many more questions and Delgado gave monosyllabic answers.

This went on for almost ten minutes before Sebastian caught doubt in Gustavo's voice, a slight hesitation. It was obvious he was posing a very delicate question.

Mrs. Delgado responded with a contained sob. Her eyes turned red and watery. Her husband closed his fist. He made a snappy retort. Sebastian could feel the coldness in the voice. The man was angry and fighting hard to contain his temper.

Another question from Gustavo and the man stood up in a flash. He pointed an accusing finger at Gustavo, every word he uttered delivered with intensity through gritted teeth. Sebastian thought they'd reached the limit and it might turn ugly.

As the woman sobbed, Gustavo rose from the sofa. "We'd better leave," he said to Sebastian, who didn't need telling twice.

Then Gustavo did something that reminded Sebastian of a high-school dare. He walked around the table and, as he shook the woman's hand, he fixed his eyes on Delgado, who returned the stare without flinching. He

147

had the look of a hawk on the verge of a kill.

Walking out the door with Sebastian on his tail, Gustavo stopped at the fence. Sebastian asked the Honduran what had gone wrong.

"I'll tell you in the car."

Sebastian wondered why Gustavo was waiting, then realized the gate had a padlock. The maid came rushing out, key in her hand. She let them out without a word.

"You think the guy spoke better English than he let on?" Sebastian asked once out of earshot inside the car.

"I don't trust him to even ask him what time it is! Did you notice how he shut her up?" The aircon blew cool fresh air as Gustavo accelerated.

"Yes, also the way he answered."

"I asked several bits about the file, birth date, about the school the boy attended. He didn't waste a word."

"What did you ask that made her cry?"

"I asked what they first did when they discovered the body."

"Not very subtle."

"I know." Gustavo made a fist then took the steering wheel again. He did not look pleased with himself.

"And then?"

"I asked why the doctor would think the boy was twelve when the documents they presented showed he was eight."

"That's when he snapped."

"Yeah. I won't translate his exact words but it had to do with our mothers."

"Ouch."

"Exactly."

They remained quiet. Sebastian digested this new development. He had a few ideas, but decided to ask the expert first. "What now?"

"Well, now I *know* he's lying, but we can't prove it. How about you?"

"I got the same feeling. I bet he abuses her too. Maybe you should check the guy's rap sheet. Can you do that?"

Gustavo nodded. "Got a friend in the police, but domestic violence is not reported or even handled in the same way as in the U.S. Wouldn't surprise me if he comes out squeaky clean, like a model citizen."

"Okay. Let's do it anyway. Also, I was looking at the pictures they had on display. Most of them were dated on the lower corner."

"Yeah, I saw them."

"One of the pictures looked like a wedding reception. She wasn't wearing a white gown but the happy face was there along with a lawyer-looking dude carrying some documents."

"Okay?" Gustavo said it like a question, expecting more to come.

Sebastian realized he and Gustavo were not on the same page. "The date was about ten years ago. The documents gave me an idea. Let's find a way to check the civil registry to see if he had any previous marriages."

"He does look older than her. Wouldn't hurt, I guess. It would be easy to check since I also have a friend there."

"For some reason, I knew you would."

CHAPTER TWENTY-FIVE

The following day, Gustavo took Sebastian to his office. He opened the door, Sebastian followed him in, and they sat on opposite sides of his desk. Gustavo enjoyed the usual thrills when closing a case and for all practical purposes, this case was done. He felt exhilarated.

"Nice office."

"Thanks. Do you want coffee?"

Sebastian nodded and Gustavo stood up. He went to the corner and poured two cups. He remembered what Bill Knox had said about Sebastian: brilliant mind trapped inside the body of a damned alcoholic. He had not seen Sebastian drinking too much while in Honduras. Hell, he thought Sebastian drank very little compared with the Latin standard of alcohol consumption.

Returning to the desk, he gave Sebastian his cup, then returned to his seat across the table, while Sebastian took a sip.

"Hmm, very good." Sebastian set the cup down.

"Thanks. Let's make the call." Picking up the receiver, Gustavo dialed the number then pushed the speaker button.

Roger Simmons answered on the second ring. "Hello."

"We're ready for the conference. I know you hate to be on speaker, but—"

"It can't be helped this time. Let me get Bill in here."

They waited for a minute before they heard the familiar Texan accent. "How you doin', fellas? Gettin' along fine?"

"We're okay, Bill. This is a nice country."

"Damn right, Sebastian. That's why we're deducting your stay from your vacation time."

While Sebastian laughed, Gustavo thought about Bill's sense of humor. Yep, joke or not, Bill always made you pay for your privileges.

Hesitant to begin, Gustavo looked at Sebastian who seemed to guess what was on his mind. The gringo nodded. "You got the info, you get to tell it."

Gustavo smiled to himself. It was nice of Sebastian to do that. It showed modesty while making people trust him. Gustavo related the facts he uncovered after the visiting the Delgado household.

"After interviewing the parents, we checked public records to find out if the father had a previous marriage or any other children."

"And?" prompted Roger.

"Records show he registered a son before. He would turn thirteen this winter. Still, maybe due to laziness or just plain stupidity, Mr. Delgado never signed up *that* child for inclusion in the insurance policy."

"I knew it!" boasted Bill. "I told ya that sucker was up to no damn good!"

Gustavo continued, "Now we must turn this over to the proper authorities."

"Yes. But that is not our job." Roger intervened. "The office that signed the policy has to follow it through."

"Okay. Then I will send you the copies of the documents we've gathered."

"Good. I'll make sure they are forwarded to the right people."

"So now I can go back home?"

"Not yet, Sebastian. I have another delicate case I want you and Gustavo to handle."

"What is it?"

"A missing person."

"The company issues insurance for missing people now?" Gustavo's question was an attempt at humorous sarcasm. He expected a reaction from Roger.

"Of course not!" Roger Simmons sounded like a professor asked by a student to change his grade. He continued in his normal voice. "It's a regular life insurance policy. The person traveled to Honduras, and then went missing. The wife needs the money and wants him declared dead before the seven years stipulated by law."

"You need a body for that," Gustavo said.

"Attaboy!" said Bill.

"We need you to follow the man's last footsteps and see what you can turn up."

"Sounds like a goose chase," said Sebastian.

"Couldn't agree more," Gustavo joined in, his feelings mutual.

Sensing his employees' rebellious mindset, Roger changed tactics. "Listen guys. This woman somehow got my direct number and she's calling me every week. I can tell she is desperate. I don't want to reach the point where I receive calls every day!"

"What do you expect us to find?" Gustavo knew Roger's bean-counter methods would not send him on a wasteful search. He had to have something up his sleeve.

"I want you to determine if the guy was just escaping."

"Like with a lover?"

"Yes."

"Why do you think that?" Sebastian asked.

"He ..." Roger hesitated.

"The sucker *borrowed* a few thousand dollars from his partners before leaving," Bill said.

"The wife hired a P.I. but he hadn't found out anything before she ran out of money."

"Where was he last seen?"

"A hotel in Tela."

"Villas Telamar?"

"You got it, Gus!"

Gustavo turned to look at Sebastian. The gringo shrugged. He was okay with it.

"Roger, please send us the most up-to-date file."

"Consider it done." He sounded relieved. The line went dead.

"Change your hotel reservation. You're going to the beach."

"Yippee." Sebastian said with the enthusiasm of an undertaker.

CHAPTER TWENTY SIX

SAN PEDRO SULA, HONDURAS

Roberto Castro did not view himself as arrogant, but he was aware that many people thought he was. His meteoric rise in the second largest bank in Honduras was a combination of ruthlessness, connections and at some point, sheer luck for being in the right place at the right time.

During business hours, he wore long-sleeved silk shirts, his gold cuff links engraved with his initials. His thick wedding ring could easily double up as a bolt nut and would sometimes set off metal detectors. At forty-two, he kept himself trim and exercised every day in a fancy gym. His hair was always combed straight back, held in place by a precise amount of gel. But his looks did not give him his reputation for arrogance; it was his treatment of others.

The job he had to do today was to drop the ax on a small legal firm. The bank president didn't want to do it because he was ashamed of the deed, and with good reason. The owner of the firm was a former top executive at the bank, who had migrated with a promise of steady work. At the time, the executive had said it felt more like a lateral move. In reality, it ran that way for a few years.

Now the bonanza days were over and the bank sought ways to cut unnecessary expenditures; the legal firm was one such case. The president had delegated the executioner's job to Roberto because of his cutthroat reputation. Roberto's ax was a settlement document now resting inside his briefcase.

He arrived at Pedro Ayala's office ten minutes ahead of the scheduled appointment. The secretary admitted him at once.

Roberto noticed Pedro did not stand up from his desk to greet him. That was a bad sign. Okay, if that's the way he wants to play it, he thought.

"Hello, Pedro. This won't take long." Roberto sat on the other side of the mahogany desk and placed the briefcase on top, unconcerned about the documents Pedro had there. He pulled out the two copies of the settlement and passed them to his host.

"What is this?" Without waiting for a response from Roberto, Pedro took the documents, put on thin reading glasses, and remained quiet for a few minutes as he read. "I won't sign this."

"The proposal is already approved and signed by the bank. I think your signature is more for proof of receipt, not your agreement to it."

"I hired you, you sonofabitch! Now you have the *nerve* to come and ditch me with this piece of crap?"

Roberto had anticipated an outburst, and come prepared with a reply. "You hired me as your hatchet man. You said so yourself." He paused for effect, then added. "I am sorry it has come to this but the global economy being what it is, the bank can't afford to have quite so many lawyers on retainer. The fact that I am coming in person to hand deliver you a settlement is in deference to your years of service."

"Oh, you make me feel so special, even when you're stabbing me in the back!" The cynicism was vintage Ayala.

"Pedro, we would prefer to end things on amicable terms."

"I bet you would. I tried to teach you to never burn bridges, but I think that is something you will never learn."

Roberto bit his tongue, he was about to say the only reason he was there was because his boss was a coward. But he stopped himself. That comment could come back to bite him in the ass. He simply sat there, staring at Pedro who stared back.

They stared at each other for what felt like several minutes, neither flinching. Roberto knew these Samurai stare-downs could go on forever and remembered Pedro Ayala had been the one who had taught him how to deal with them.

Pedro remained seated during the exchange. Now that tension had escalated, any fool would think a standing position – higher ground – would provide an advantage. Roberto was smart enough to not succumb to that illusion, no matter how tempting in this instance. He knew that as Pedro spoke last, he was on the spot and could not continue to stare back at the seated bastard. Pedro was smug, but not unbreakable.

"I said this would not take long. I can leave this and send somebody to pick it up at your convenience but I was hoping we could wrap it up. You've always said you hated to drag things out without reason."

Pedro smiled at the last line. He stopped looking at Roberto and lowered his gaze to the document in front of him. In complete silence and with a single fluid motion, he took his Montblanc fountain pen from his shirt pocket, initialed the first two pages, and signed the last one. Then did the same with the second set.

He returned the pen to its original place and slid the first set of documents toward his visitor.

Roberto had a difficult time controlling his elation. He had expected this meeting to be more dramatic and he had prepared a few more lines; evil ones, smart insults.

Now they would remain unsaid.

Then he understood. By giving him this early victory, Pedro had stolen the glory. Pedro had signed to spite him.

In one swift motion, Pedro had stolen Roberto's thunder, the limelight, the chance to humiliate Pedro any more. Smug bastard!

With nothing more to do, Roberto placed the document inside the briefcase and turned to leave, not bothering to bid farewell.

* * * *

When Roberto opened the car door, he felt something hard, cold and metallic pressed against the base of his nape. He went rigid.

"Get in," said a gruff voice.

Roberto tried to turn to see his assailant but harder pressure on his neck convinced him to desist. He rushed to get in. The man leaned in the gap between the open door and the car and pressed the button on the armrest to unlock the other doors. At once, the front passenger door opened and another man brandishing a gun climbed in, allowing the first one to close the driver's door and get in the back.

"If you do as we tell you, you'll be out alive in thirty minutes."

Roberto felt cold sweat trickling down his back.

"Start the car. Get us out of here."

With his heart beating faster than it would after twenty intense minutes of cardio in the expensive gym the company paid for, Roberto started the engine. He backed out of the parking bay and drove ahead. He stopped at the gate, not knowing where to go.

"It's a one way street, dude. Turn left!" said the gunman next to him.

He sped up. Only then did Roberto remember he had made a maintenance appointment for the following day

– he liked to keep his new SUV in prime condition. Following what he thought was a random pattern, Roberto drove around major avenues amidst the heavy noon traffic. Except for the driving instructions, the two men kept quiet.

The one in the front sat straight while the one sitting in the back leaned forward, his gun fixed on Roberto's lower right side.

"How much longer?" asked the gunman in the back.

"We are getting close." He turned to face Roberto. "Don't worry, you'll get out soon. Do you have satellite tracking?"

"No," Roberto lied. He had installed it the same week he got the car. He was pushing fifty miles per hour over the highway that led to Puerto Cortes when the gunman told him to pull over.

"This is your stop."

Roberto stepped out, then the man in the back moved into the driver's seat. He closed the door and powered down the window.

"Cell phone, wallet, watch … those fancy things on your sleeves … and the ring."

Enraged, Roberto did not move. He'd had his wedding ring for almost ten years. He did not want to part with it. He looked defiant, but then he saw the gun pointed straight at his face. The man cocked the hammer. Roberto gave it all up.

"We'd better not hear anything on the police frequency until tomorrow or we'll come back for you. Is that clear?" Roberto nodded as the men sped off leaving him standing in the middle of the road.

Usually considered a busy highway, Roberto surmised his assailants had calculated when the road would be quiet.

The sun was high, shining bright. He had no money and there were no passing cars. He crossed the median

158

strip and walked back toward the city.

After five minutes walking, his silk shirt was drenched and stuck to his back. He had not walked in the sun since his high school years. He was used to exercise in the comfort of an air-conditioned gym or the in the privacy of his home. The upside was that he was not out of breath.

He dwelled on his lost possessions. The alligator leather wallet had been a Christmas present; his seven-hundred-dollar Bulova wristwatch was not irreplaceable either, although he loved that particular style. He wondered if he could still get the same model. The cufflinks and wedding band were the only jewelry he ever used. What else was in the car?

"Oh shit!" He remembered the briefcase in the backseat.

As a reflex action, he turned to look in the direction the car had gone. It was useless.

He cursed some more as he turned back and resumed walking. He heard an engine noise grow louder. He turned in time to see the taxi and flagged it down.

* * * *

Roberto Castro walked into the great hall of the bank. His pace was brisk. He reached a high table with a guest telephone, much like those in a hotel. He had thought of the design for the bank's foyer when he saw it for the first time. He dialed his own office extension.

His secretary picked up after the first ring. He summed up what he had been through in two quick sentences. "Now I need to borrow two hundred Lempiras to pay the cab," he finished.

"Of course, Mr. Castro. I'll come right down."

True to her word, she arrived as soon as the elevator could deliver her and gave him the money. He went out to pay his fare and returned. They took the elevator to his office together.

"What do you want to do now?"

"I don't care much about the car, it has insurance. However, my briefcase with the Ayala documents was in it."

"Oh no!"

"I'm sure that asshole will refuse to sign again, just to spite me."

When the elevator reached their floor, she went to her desk and called the head of security as he had requested.

Roberto went inside the office suite. They had taken his favorite set of cufflinks but he had not rolled up his sleeves yet, confident that he had an extra set in his desk's top drawer. After checking all the drawers, he remembered he took the extra set to a jewelry store for polishing.

Swearing, he stood up and went to the small cupboard where he kept a backpack with gym clothes. He unzipped it and pulled out a white T-shirt. He looked at it, holding it up. He pictured himself wearing it over his dress pants.

"Oh damn it!" He threw the T-shirt back inside and rolled up his sleeves.

The head of security arrived and Roberto filled him in.

"We have to go to the police station to make the statement and we call the security guys to turn on the GPS tracking system."

"They told me they'd kill me if I went to the police today."

"Maybe it was a bluff to make you comply."

"I'm not willing to take that risk. It's my life on the line, not yours!"

"Your call."

"Can't you talk to the tracking guys to activate the service without the police report?"

"I'll try."

Roberto asked his secretary make the call and patch it through to his desk. The security man spoke for about a minute explaining the delicate situation. He listened for a couple of seconds.

"Isn't it something you can do?" the security man pleaded, then added, "We do have many cars registered with you."

He listened for another minute. His grimace told Roberto the answer: they wouldn't do it.

"Hold on a minute."

"What?" Roberto looked up.

"I have an idea. I think they said no to me because they don't know me, but maybe they would do it for somebody else."

"Somebody else?"

"Somebody they've worked with. Let me go back to my office and check my files to see who made the initial contact."

"Whatever it takes."

* * * *

"Yes?" came the voice of Pedro Ayala in Roberto's office speakerphone.

The head of security had come back with the news that Mr. Ayala had been the initial contact with the security office. When asked to intervene, the curt denial came accompanied with the advice to ask Roberto Castro about the reasons.

"Pedro, I need your help with GPS Tracking Services."

A brief silence. "What do you want?"

Roberto sighed then told Pedro about his ordeal. He was careful to leave out the final details about the cell phone, the wallet, and above all, the briefcase. He felt the stare from the security guy. He was not sure if it was admiration, or awe, at his gall in asking for help to retrieve the proverbial dagger, only to stab it into Ayala's back again.

"Alerting the police is part of their protocol."

"I know!" Roberto heard the strain on his voice. It sounded like a squeak. He cleared his throat before speaking again. "I already told you I can't do that."

"You can't? Maybe you're just afraid to do it." Pablo delivered the line as a single monotone sentence. No hint of sneer, cynicism, or reproach.

Roberto remembered reading that revenge was a dish better served cold. But he felt Pedro had microwaved his. It was a standoff. He understood that Pedro expected him to beg for help.

The silence rivaled that of a respectful minute to mourn the dead. As if that was the case, Pedro broke the spell after about fifty seconds.

"I'll see what I can do. Call me again in five minutes." The line went dead.

Seven minutes later, Roberto rushed down the elevator with the head of security. The latter was barking orders on his radio to have a company SUV ready.

They boarded the back seat and the car sped off. An armed guard sat on the front seat along with the driver. Both of them wore bulletproof vests over their blue uniform shirts.

Reaching into the back, the chief pulled out two more vests. He handed one to Roberto and pulled one over his shirt. Roberto did the same; he hadn't expected the vest to be so heavy. The chief adjusted the side Velcro straps for a better fit, but too tight.

"Is it supposed to inhibit my breathing?"

"On the contrary, it is meant to keep you breathing." He grinned and adjusted the straps until Roberto could breathe properly. "Sir, I still don't think you need to tag along."

"Oh, but I have to." It may have been the adrenaline

rush, or the fear of failure, he wasn't sure, but Roberto could not stay behind to wait for a report. Despite the danger, Roberto had to have that briefcase.

They drove out of the bank and took a southern course. The chief answered his ringing phone. He nodded a few times and then hung up.

"Airport," he said.

The driver turned in the next available street, the abrupt change in direction almost toppling Roberto on top of the chief. After more turns and what Roberto thought could be a Nascar record, they entered the highway that led to the airport. In another five minutes, they made a right turn into a middle-class suburb. The streets were wide but had speed bumps on every corner. Their vehicle anchored up for each hump after the passengers hit the roof while jumping the previous one. They took a side street, then a very narrow one that had enough room for one car. After four houses, there was an empty lot on the left. There a blue and black Prado stood.

"That is not your license plate," said the chief.

"But it's my car. There," he pointed, "behind the back door is a scratch my wife made with a supermarket trolley."

"Let's proceed with caution."

The driver parked the car before reaching the empty lot. The three armed security men approached the parked car with their weapons drawn.

163

CHAPTER TWENTY SEVEN

TELA, HONDURAS

Howard Gonzales ran his car theft operations like a military maneuver. He was the commander, monitoring every step from his base via cell phone and backup two-way radios.

He paced up and down while Carlos hunched over his laptop accessing the dealer's database for a full report on the car's maintenance. A scanner monitored the police band. No one had reported the Prado missing so far.

"Marcos, have you changed the plates yet?" he said into his phone.

"Yes."

"And where is Gregorio?"

"He's with my car waiting for us beyond the toll gate."

"Good."

"We are ready to go ... wait!" Marcos's voice sounded worried.

"What is it?"

"A car just parked behind us. It's a white suburban. Tinted windows."

"Damn!"

"Three men got out. Shit! They have guns!"

"Tell Pablo to drive out of there!" Howard ordered.

"No. Let them get closer."

Howard did not like to be contradicted. On the other hand, Marcos was on site and he could not second-guess his decision. He accepted the change in plans on the assumption Marcos knew what he was doing. He held his breath all the while.

"Now!" he heard Marcos scream to Pablo.

The loud roar of the engine reverberated through the connection. They were on the move.

"What's happening?" He could hear Marcos laughing.

"Like I thought, they hesitated to take a shot. Now they are running back to their car. They will come after us but we have a head start."

"Good job. Now finish it and lose them for good!"

"Roger that."

"How did they find it?" Carlos looked up from his computer screen.

"Marcos, did you check the car for GPS?" Howard said.

"The guy said there wasn't one."

"Did it occur to you he might be lying?" He felt like biting off Marcos's head.

"He almost shat in his pants. I didn't think—"

"Well, obviously shitty-pants lied to you!" Howard cursed in frustration, and then snapped at Carlos. "Get on that laptop of yours and disable it!"

"I can't do that."

"What!"

"Well," Carlos began, "I can't turn the tracking device on and off. The security firm has a very secure website."

"Then what good are you!" All of a sudden, he did not feel as confident in the people surrounding him.

* * * *

The three men rushed back to the car. The driver started the engine and took off without a word. Roberto realized they had wasted precious seconds by not having left the car engine on idle.

It was not the first time the driver had participated in high-speed chases judging by the hard turns and

165

screeching tires, until they glimpsed the rear bumper of the Prado as it swerved to the left. They were gaining. Roberto flinched at seeing his car driven at breakneck speed.

"Can you take the shot?" The security chief brought Roberto out of his reverie.

"Yes." The guard in the front seat lowered the window and eased out half his body, and sat on the edge.

Through the windshield, Roberto saw the extended arm and the handgun, surprised at how steady it looked. Then he heard the first shot. He thought he saw a flash of light an inch above the Prado's rear tire.

Roberto leaned forward for a better look at the extended arm trained on his car. He was not thrilled at the thought of his car being bullet-riddled. Then he remembered he was not after the car but the documents.

A second flash from the muzzle. Jackpot.

* * * *

"What was that?" asked Howard.

"They're shooting at us."

"Take evasive actions. Do not engage."

"Copy. Don't agree but will carry on."

"They shot the tire!"

"Damn!" Howard looked at Carlos, still hunched over his computer. The wizard's hands moved over the keyboard at speed.

Howard considered his options. If caught, Marcos would keep quiet. He was not sure about Pablo. If apprehended, Marcos had instructions to treat Pablo as a risk. Still, he did not want Marcos to go to jail either. It would increase the chances of uncovering his organization. A large part of his success was that he had stayed below the radar.

His next order was unusual. He prided himself that few were hurt on his operations. Okay, there was the occasional 'collateral damage', but he hated it every time.

166

"Engage. Go for the engine, do not use lethal force."

"Understood." Not a few seconds later, he heard two shots in rapid succession. "Done. I hit the engine block. They are pulling over."

"I got it!" Carlos jumped up from his desk.

"You got what?"

"I told you I can't disable the device but I hacked into the company database and found where they hid it." He looked proud in a childish way, as if he expected a teacher to place a gold star on his forehead.

"What good is that?"

"We could take it out, or smash it. Anything," he said, sounding peevish because his breakthrough did not garner the reward he had anticipated.

"Marcos, did you hear that?"

"Where is it?" said the man through the speaker-phone.

"It is beneath the rug under the back seat."

After a short pause, Marcos spoke again. "Got it."

"Turn the jammer on, get rid of it and call us back," Howard was not taking anything for granted with Marcos anymore.

"Roger and out."

* * * *

Roberto Castro paced up and down the car. A column of steam shot up, hissing out of the engine.

"I thought this car was bullet proof." He was furious.

The chief was in the middle of a heated argument over the phone, but he stopped for a second to reply. "Lucky shot."

"You think?"

The chief resumed his conversation; after another machine-gun battery of curses, he placed a hand to cover the receiver and turned to Roberto. "They located the car."

"What took so long?"

"They don't know and gave me the run around. But now they are able to pinpoint the car's location again. It is near here."

"We need to get there."

"I'm on it." He turned toward the phone again.

Still, Roberto did not trust his chief anymore. He thought of a Plan B. He pulled out the cell phone he had taken from his secretary and dialed the bank's switchboard, then entered the extension. Roberto asked her to have a car ready for him but to wait for his signal.

A white pickup truck pulled up alongside them and lowered the window. By the chief's demeanor, Roberto figured it must be another of his guards. The four stranded men boarded the new vehicle. Roberto sat wedged between the first driver and the chief.

They rode for a few minutes, taking the main road again. They turned at the little suburb of Calpules, then followed an unpaved street. Roberto had never visited this part of town. He'd heard about it but had never cared to venture in. At the end of one long street, they pulled over.

"This time we'll do it the right way," said the chief. "You two go around the block and come from the other end." Then he turned to the first driver. "You come with me."

The two who had ridden in the front broke into a run going back the way they had come. Roberto's gaze followed their backs until they turned the corner and were out of sight. The chief and the first driver checked their weapons. Two minutes later, the chief's cell phone beeped. He pulled it out and read the text message.

"They're in position."

They climbed out of the truck and walked around the corner, weapons drawn. Roberto stayed behind. He moved behind the wheel and this time made sure the engine was running.

He could not sit still, anxiety tormenting him. He craned his neck trying to see more but the high fence of a construction company blocked his view. He drummed his fingers on the wheel. He pulled out the cell phone and stared at it. He put the phone on the dashboard. Drummed some more then took the phone and looked at it again. Not even a minute had passed by.

Roberto got out, walked to the corner, and popped his head around the edge to see what was happening. The four men hunched over an old battered Toyota Corolla. Roberto looked all around but saw no sign of his Prado. Could they be at the wrong place?

The chief bent down and picked up something from the floor, then all four men started toward the corner, their faces contorted with disbelief. When they came close, the Chief extended his hand so Roberto could look. It was a black plastic rectangular box, about three inches long by an inch wide, with no distinctive markings.

"This is the transmitter. They make it innocuous so they're hard to find during a general search." The chief turned it over; it had two small circles, one on each end. "The other side has magnets."

Roberto frowned. "It was meant to be well hidden."

The chief shrugged. He looked baffled, defeated. Roberto sighed, he was about to start screaming about incompetence when he heard a car pull up behind him. When he turned around, he saw Pedro Ayala sporting a benevolent smile through the back window of a white SUV. He signaled Roberto to come closer.

As he drew nearer, Pedro said, "Hop in. I'll take you back to the bank."

"No, thank you." Who did he think he was! Roberto wondered.

"Oh, come on. Do you really want to ride back with those two armed blockheads who could not find your car?" His tone was bordering on cynical, but then added, *sotto voce,* "I'm guessing they'll be out of a job tomorrow."

"I prefer to take a taxi." Roberto could not bear to feel so vanquished in front of his former mentor.

"And have your secretary pay for the ride again?"

Roberto also wondered how Pedro could know so much. Did he have an informer in the bank? Roberto looked straight into the man's eyes. The rest of his face was grave, but calm. That damn twinkle in the eyes convinced him Pedro was enjoying this.

Halfheartedly, Roberto walked around the car and got in on the other side. Reluctant to admit defeat, he told himself he accepted the ride to try to discover Pedro's spy.

The car's interior smelled of new leather. The quiet air conditioner cooled the interior to luxurious comfort. Pedro powered up the tinted window, blocking the daylight and giving the interior a sense of dark privacy. The eerie silence added to the effect.

The car moved forward and Roberto looked through the window on his side as they passed houses and small businesses. He felt isolated, defenseless. He hated every second of it.

"I brought you something." Pedro said.

He turned and saw a manila envelope in Pedro's hand.

"Take it."

After he took the envelope, Roberto pulled out the contents. He gasped when he realized he held a notarized photocopy of the contract Pedro Ayala had signed that morning.

"I figured you'd lost your original when I heard about the tenacity with which you were going after the car. It was reckless of you to go after armed thieves over a document! Lucky they hit the car instead of the window,

170

or you."

Roberto overcame his emotion and found his voice. "Why are you giving me this?"

"I'm saving you the trouble of asking for it."

Roberto looked away from Pedro, pondering this.

"Do you want to know a secret?" This made Roberto turn back. "My business has grown exponentially over the last three years. I've made several investments that made good returns. Our little contract with the bank was peanuts in comparison. On top of that, it was also a burden because of all the resources I had to allocate to a single account."

"You want the settlement to take effect." It all looked so clear now.

Pedro Ayala nodded. They rode in silence the rest of the way. Roberto felt not only humiliated, but outsmarted. He should have seen this coming. He should have kept an eye on his vendor's finances, or at least looked at it before making the offer.

In the end, he had done Pedro a favor; albeit a costly one because of the president's guilt about going back on his word.

They reached the bank and Roberto stepped out. When he was about the close the door, he leaned over and asked, "Did you set me up?" The idea crossed his mind at the last instant.

Pedro laughed and shook his head. "No. I leave filthy stunts like that to backstabbing bastards like you."

Chapter Twenty Eight

San Pedro Sula, Honduras

The next day, Sebastian checked out of the hotel, and Gustavo drove them to Tela.

The road started as a four-lane boulevard that ran all the way to a city named El Progreso. After that was a single lane of black asphalt. The side of the road varied from small houses to green patches of vegetation. He caught glimpses of banana trees, high mountains with virgin vegetation, then palm trees.

Gustavo told him about a large company in San Alejo which processed palm oil; the plantation they were driving by at that moment, was one of the largest.

"You have a beautiful country." He could not keep his eyes off the landscape. It all belonged on postcards.

"Yeah. Lots of green."

"Exactly. I've never seen so many different shades of green."

"And yet, we're not listed as a 'green' country."

The comment brought a laugh from Sebastian. Gustavo's sense of humor was growing on him.

"Listen. I've been meaning to ask you. What was all that political mess a couple of years ago?"

"It was nothing but a three-ring circus. Bottom line, a bunch of people didn't agree with the direction the president was taking, so they removed him."

"Was that legal?"

"Depends on whom you ask."

Very diplomatic, thought Sebastian. He was curious to hear his host's point of view. "I'm asking you."

Gustavo hesitated before replying. "Borderline gray area." He fell silent for a moment, as if considering what to say next. "In hindsight I think it was a good plan ... great execution but lousy follow up. The country was hammered by the international community."

"Can't blame them. It can't be much fun when they see one of their political counterparts sent into exile."

"You gringos are very naïve. I bet you think Lee Harvey Oswald shot Kennedy."

"As a matter of fact, I do." Upon arriving in Dallas, he had visited the scene of the shooting. He went upstairs into the book depository and looked down from the window. He thought the explanations given were pretty accurate. At least they felt truthful. He did not elaborate, but instead said to Gustavo, "It is far easier to believe the crap about the conspiracy theory than to accept that a single man could kill a president."

"There you go ... we have the same situation here. It was easier to name it a *coup d'état* than to admit some angry people decided to take out the trash."

Sebastian considered the last comment. "You got me there."

They were quiet until Gustavo changed the subject. "How was it, working for the Fire Department?"

"I thought the department was my life for almost fifteen years. I was proved wrong when I lost my family. They were my real life."

"Losing dear ones is never easy. Bill didn't tell me specifics. Do you mind if I ask how they died?"

"Air crash." Sebastian didn't feel like elaborating.

"Bill mentioned something about you not liking to fly. I guess that makes sense."

"It's not fear. It's memories haunting me."

"That's why you drank on the flight down here?"

"Only way to cope."

"Got it." Gustavo kept his eye on the road ahead.

Sebastian was surprised to learn his excessive drinking showed the first time he met Gustavo. Then he remembered what happened later at the hotel and smiled. He said, "Then you tried to get me into bed with a hooker."

"I guess you weren't drunk enough then." Gustavo smiled. "By the way, I'm sorry about that. We got off to a bad start."

"It's okay. I know you meant no harm."

Gustavo looked ahead; his expression suggested he was thinking how to move away from shaky ground. After a while he added, "For what is worth, it won't happen again."

Sebastian smiled. "I know."

The construction on the side of the road became denser. Gustavo slowed down and made a left turn, then followed a narrow street. Many pedestrians and people on bikes populated the way around the small town. They crossed what looked like a very old and neglected railroad.

Sebastian remembered something he had read before, "I thought there was no rail system in the country."

"Not anymore. It used to run all across the banana plantations on the North Coast, all the way to Puerto Cortés."

"It's a shame. I like trains. They're reliable."

"I'll take your word for it. I've never been on one."

They followed a street that ran parallel to the coast; the palm trees swayed in the wind. Ahead, they reached a property with a low white fence. Behind it, houses rose high on pylons. Sometimes with a cement base underneath, the houses, made out of wood, were painted light green, baby blue, or yellow with white corners, with zinc roofs.

"That's the hotel complex." Gustavo pointed to the

right.

"Looks big."

"About two miles long. It used to be the residential complex of the Tela Railroad Company then turned into a hotel back in the early eighties."

They reached a break in the fence and Gustavo duly turned into it. A barrier with a counterweight prevented entry though the barrier. A guard holding a clipboard appeared from the small gate room. He approached them on the driver's side and Gustavo lowered his window.

"Welcome to Telamar. How can we help you?" The guard was polite and businesslike.

Sebastian liked hotels that were serious about security.

"We come to see Sargento Mendoza."

"Your name, please."

"Gustavo Fonseca." He produced his driver's license and handed it to the guard.

The man checked the clipboard. They had been announced.

Gustavo turned to Sebastian. "I think he's going to need yours, too."

Sebastian pulled his driver's license out and handed it over, too. The guard kept their identification and provided them with clip badges that marked them as *Visitantes*.

Following the guard's directions, Gustavo drove into the complex and turned into a parking area designated for special visitors or vendors. Hotel guests had designated parking places further into the complex.

Sergeant Mendoza's desk was in the far right corner of the room with a gunmetal gray file cabinet behind him; paperwork and folders almost hid the desk.

After the formal introductions, they settled on speaking English for Sebastian's benefit.

"As you know, we are here to follow up on the disap-

175

pearance of Frank Meyer," Gustavo said.

"From the insurance company, correct?" Mendoza spoke with a heavy accent.

"Yes. Any problem with that?"

"No. I don't receive these enquiries very often. After you called me yesterday, I contacted Mrs. Meyer and she told me to cooperate in any way I could. She was not sure if they were sending actual insurance people or external representatives."

"I am a direct employee of the agency," said Sebastian.

"And I'm on retainer when they need a local set of eyes."

Mendoza nodded. "Okay, that's clear. Let's move on."

"What can you tell us? Start at the beginning, please."

Mendoza took a folder from the top of one of the neat piles stacked on his desk. He opened the file containing several pages, bound by a metal fastener. Sebastian smothered a smile concerning the military efficiency of Sergeant Mendoza.

"Mr. Meyer checked in on Thursday, February second," he read from the file. "His original reservation was for four nights. He signed a credit card voucher. On Saturday morning, Housekeeping reported his room had been unused."

"Unused?" Sebastian asked.

Mendoza lifted his gaze to see him. "Yes. Unused, not slept in. The bed covers were intact."

"But that can't be all that unusual. I mean, he could sleep in somebody else's room, party all night, or something like that. Right?"

"Of course," Mendoza smiled. "That is not something to worry about, but Housekeeping makes a report anyway. The bags were still there, and we left everything as it was. Then she reported the same situation the following day. We took action on the third day.

176

"I accompanied the head of Housekeeping into the room. We searched for some contact information or some clue that might explain his absence."

"At what point did you call the police?" Gustavo asked.

"That same day. Our initial search bore no result, so we called the police. They searched the room, too, with a person from hotel security and housekeeping present all the time. Nothing."

"Then?"

Mendoza sat back and sighed. He shrugged. "Police did some snooping around I gather, but that was it."

"Who contacted Mrs. Meyer?"

"Front Desk Manager. She speaks better English," he explained after seeing Gustavo's frown.

"What happened next?"

"Well, when the voucher reached its limit, we had to vacate the guestroom. We made an inventory of the room's content, bagged everything, and placed it in a locked warehouse."

"Understandable. You guys need the room." Sebastian commented. "Do you still have it here?"

"I'm afraid not. Mrs. Meyer requested we send it to her by courier."

"Bummer."

"We took digital pictures of the room. Would you like to see them?"

"That would be very helpful." Gustavo said.

Mendoza produced the pictures. There were over twenty of them. He divided them into two stacks, and gave one to each visitor.

Sebastian sorted through his pile. The room seemed standard. Two beds with the covers intact, a credenza with a flat-screen TV, a writing desk in the far corner, a jacket on the back of the chair. He saw palm leaves and patches of white sand through the French doors.

You could tell a lot from a man's traveling habits. Sebastian would dress from a suitcase placed near the bathroom. Frank Meyer's fastidiousness showed on the pictures of the closet: two pairs of pants on the left, two long-sleeved shirts in the middle and two short-sleeved on the right. A pair of polished black dress shoes on the floor, the high shine reflecting the flash. Gustavo must have been having similar thoughts for he showed him a picture of the bathroom with all the toiletries neatly arranged on the right side of the sink.

"Wow," he muttered.

"Yeah. This guy thinks everything through," Gustavo said.

"Something's odd." Sebastian recalled reading the file on the way; Frank Meyer had taken a large sum of money from his partners and arrived at San Pedro Sula. The next day he took a bus to Tela and registered at Telamar. He found it odd that a person with this level of meticulousness would just jump ship. It did not feel right. He began to see why Mrs. Meyer persisted in bugging the hell out of Simmons.

"Can we see if he had any visitors?" Gustavo asked after a moment.

"Sure. All visitors must be announced. In fact, they cannot go into the hotel. The guest must receive them at the Reception building."

"Like we were today?"

Mendoza nodded, "Or else pay an entry fee. Let me get the log book." He rose from the desk and went across the room to where a row of six four-drawer file cabinets stood side by side. Mendoza knew what he was looking for and where to find it. He opened one of the drawers and pulled out a legal-sized logbook. He returned to his desk and flipped through the pages.

"Here." His index finger stayed on a line. "A Mr. Jimmy James Costly visited him on Friday."

"Did the police follow up on visitors?"

"Yes, I have a mark here that this page was photocopied and turned over to them."

"Then that's probably a dead end anyway."

"Only when you reach the end," said Sebastian, remembering Bill Knox's attitude toward anything he didn't check all the way through.

"Now you sound like Bill!" Gustavo added with a laugh. "Okay, let's follow the lead." Then to Mendoza, "Can you arrange for us to meet with the police? It is better if we have a referral, you know."

"Of course. Let me make a phone call and I'll get back to you."

With nothing to do for the next couple of hours, they walked across the street to the lobby. Sebastian could tell this building was new. Its design alone stood out. The shape was akin to a chalet, but bigger. The front and side walls were traditional French doors and windows with tinted glass panels.

Inside, the ceiling was so high there could have been a mezzanine floor. A partition hung from the ceiling to a meter above an elevated desk, creating the appearance of a window in the Reception area.

Above the reception desk, on the partition, hung several oil paintings. A large one, Sebastian guessed six by four feet, dominated the center. It showed a jungle, with a red macaw prominent in the lower right corner and other wild animals scattered around the landscape. All bordered by a four-inch ornate wood frame. Sebastian's gaze lingered a few seconds on each painting but there were too many of them, almost making it cluttered. In the foremost left corner, a different kind of artifact caught his attention. He made a mental note to ask Mendoza about it.

Two women behind the reception desk registered them within minutes.

Once in his room, Sebastian recognized it as the same layout he had seen in the Meyer pictures. The same flat-screen TV hung on the wall, same writing desk in the corner.

The only difference was the view from the balcony. His room was on the second floor, so there was no sand this time. Instead, he had a view of the palm tops as they swayed to the whims of the wind.

The white phone on the night table rang. It was Gustavo to tell him he had arranged a meeting with the head of Housekeeping in twenty minutes' time in the open bar by the beach.

He took a quick shower to freshen up from sitting in the car for the long journey. He put on khaki shorts, a white linen shirt, and sandals, before he went out.

He followed a path that led him to a white picket fence. Beyond the fence was nothing but fine white sand, short palm trees, and the horizon where the line between the ocean and the sky blurred. He took the boardwalk that led to the oversized gazebo that served as the bar.

Along the way, he encountered vendors selling coconut bread, some ocean-themed fantasy jewelry, and a small girl offering to braid his hair for ten dollars.

He found Fonseca waiting for him. Gustavo took a swig of a Corona and placed the bottle on the table before he stood up to greet him. "Damned heat," he said in mock explanation for the beer.

Sebastian smiled and sat across from him, which left him a view of the bar rather than the ocean. He grimaced and moved his chair next to Gustavo, so he could enjoy the landscape. He ordered a beer for himself. They were halfway through the second beer when the housekeeper showed up.

She introduced herself as Ana Chicas before she sat with them. She was jovial the whole time, and her black bob swung every time she tilted her head. Her side of the story turned out to be a carbon copy of what Mendoza had already told them. Except she complemented it with a tale from her past that proved Frank Meyer had not been her first case of a guest gone missing.

Some five years before while she worked in a hotel in La Ceiba, she found the guest room unused for two consecutive nights. She reported it in the same fashion as she had here in Telamar; a week later, she'd recognized the missing man's face on the cover of a local newspaper. The corpse had been found bound with signs of torture. The report said the coroner suggested the body had been ditched from a moving vehicle because of the scrapes and injuries. She crossed herself and prayed Mr. Meyer had not come to a similar end.

As she finished, Victor Mendoza joined them. "All set up. The detective will see us tomorrow morning at nine."

"That leaves us nothing to do until then," Gustavo said. He signaled the waiter for another round. He asked their hosts but both refused.

"Victor, I have a favor to ask." Sebastian remembered what he had seen.

"Tell me."

"Back at reception I noticed a security camera. I wonder if you still have the video feed."

"You want to see Mr. Meyer's guest, right?" Sebastian nodded. "We keep the records for six months or so. It is motion-activated so it varies. Let me review it and see what we have."

"Thank you."

The much-deserved beers arrived and they clinked the bottles in a toast. Gustavo had been right about one thing: the damned heat was more bearable with a cold beer.

CHAPTER TWENTY NINE

TELA, HONDURAS

Howard Gonzales woke up with a scream, his heart pounding inside his chest. Without even realizing it, his right hand touched the eagle-shaped burn on his left one.

"What is it?" A female voice came from his right.

He did not recognize it. A light went on, and he turned to see her naked back as she leaned over the night lamp. Her brownish skin had a soft glow. The white bed sheet slid down, exposing her buttocks, and a thin line of a lighter shade around her waist showed her preference for thongs.

She turned back to face him, her round breasts bouncing, as if happy, like jello. The round darker areolas had small nipples. Her blonde shoulder-length hair fell untangled; an inch of black at the roots revealed its true coloring. As the fog dissipated in his head, he remembered choosing her from a lineup. He always picked the fresh younger ones. He would not bed them in the whorehouse. He paid the extra fee and went to a motel, a different one each time, where he could lock doors and not be caught with his pants down. Literally.

This girl, Telma as he recalled, stared at him. She must have been asleep too.

"Just a bad dream."

"I know the perfect cure for that." She curved her full lips into a naughty smile. She laid her hand on his chest, then circled his nipple with her index finger.

"I'm here for the entire night," she whispered in his ear. She lowered her hand as she continued to smile.

She might be under-age but was already a pro at lovemaking. The other reason Howard liked his whores young was for their eagerness to perform. Older ones were tired and would just do as they were told and demand more money for every kinky thing. Old bitches lacked the enthusiasm of rookies.

His heart, which had begun to calm down, raised tempo again but for a more pleasurable reason. He sighed as he leaned back on the bed.

Telma continued to caress him with both hands now, her fingertips touching his skin everywhere and lingering nowhere, in a continuous, almost ballet-like motion, her touch sending electric waves through his body. She moved closer and rested her lips where her hand had touched first. She stopped, looked up to him.

"Leave the light on," he said, guessing her question.

She resumed her craft as he began to moan in utter ecstasy, enjoying the view from his vantage point.

CHAPTER THIRTY

TELA, HONDURAS

Gustavo woke up with a slight headache. Mendoza would take them to see his police friend this morning and Gustavo wanted to have breakfast before that.

He dropped to the floor to do five sets of twenty push-ups. Without stopping to catch his breath, he flipped and followed with crunches. The exercise accentuated his throbbing headache, but he worked through his daily routine.

"I should have stuck with beer!" He massaged his temples on his way to the bathroom.

A cold shower, two cups of strong black coffee, without sugar, and he was ready. He walked across the corridor to Sebastian's room. He knocked but heard nothing. He rapped louder.

"Coming!"

We're cranky this morning, Gustavo thought.

Together they went to the main restaurant. The sea breeze was great with a beer in the open bar the day before – but for breakfast while suffering with hangovers – they needed aircon.

They ate while discussing the new lead. Gustavo wondered why the police had not questioned the visitor before, or maybe they did and it was a dead end. On the other hand, Roger Simmons would tear him a new one if he did not follow through on every lead, even if a faint one.

Of course, that was not the only reason. During his years in the military, he'd learned to work in a professional manner, even with the menial duties. Now that he was an independent assessor on a retainer from three major insurance companies, he would conduct himself in the same professional way.

Victor Mendoza arrived with military punctuality and the three of them walked to the parking lot. They rode to the station in Victor's car because his sedan had four doors. Sebastian's long legs decreed he rode in the front.

The small police station was located in downtown Tela and a patrol car and two police bikes occupied the front parking area. They rode half a block down the busy street until Mendoza located a spot and parked, from where they walked back to the station.

Along the sidewalks, many pedestrians went about their business. Sandals, short sleeves, and even shorts seemed to be the appropriate way to dress in the coastal city. Gustavo, Victor and Sebastian, all wearing woven pants, shoes and button-down shirts appeared out of place.

They reached the station and after a few minutes of watching Mendoza wave and say hello to people they went into a large room with two desks, but instead of facing each other like partners' desk, they both faced the door. Each had a high-back chair behind it and two chairs facing. Sebastian borrowed one from the other desk and the three sat before the inspector.

The man wore full uniform, short sleeved, his badge hanging from his neck by a chain. He introduced himself as Inspector Perez. His English was negligible, so they agreed Gustavo would translate for Sebastian. Inspector Perez checked the file he had on hand and informed them of what he knew about the investigation. They had contacted Mrs. Meyer and learned she knew nothing about the real purpose of his trip. After a week, they had turned up nothing.

At that moment, the occupant of the other desk entered the room. He nodded by way of greeting and sat at his desk. He turned to his computer and they heard a *clack-clack*-ing, as if, instead of a keyboard, he used an ancient typewriter.

"Did you follow up on his visitor?" Victor asked.

He nodded, "Nothing there. Jimmy James Costly was a dead end."

At the mention of the name, the other policeman turned with a look of disbelief on his face. "Did you just say Jimmy James Costly?"

"Yes. Why?"

In response, the man opened a drawer in his desk, browsed with his index finger and pulled out a file. Then he stood up and spread the contents of his file on top of Perez's desk.

"His mother reported him missing two weeks ago."

"¿*Que pasó?*" Sebastian said. "Well, that's the extent of my knowledge of Spanish."

The previous night Gustavo had taught him some basic lines, and asking what happened was one of them.

Gustavo held up his hand. "Let me translate to my friend before you continue." Then he turned to Sebastian and summed the situation up in three short sentences.

"No way!" was his response.

Two hours later when they had returned to the hotel, Victor excused himself.

"No problem. You've done enough," Sebastian thanked him.

"Yes, we understand you do have things to do other than run around chasing ghosts," added Gustavo.

"Well, I have a pressing matter to attend to, but I am curious about how this will turn out."

"We'll keep you posted." Sebastian promised.

* * * *

Sebastian sat on one of the easy chairs in the pool area. This part, he learned from the brochure in his room, was a new addition. The pool resembled a gigantic number eight, although a bit lopsided.

He sat at one end by the snack bar. He despised fancy bars that charged top dollar but were cheap when pouring the alcohol, but the margarita in his hand had a generous amount of tequila. The downside was that the cup was hard plastic; a glass would be better to hold the salt on the rim. Life was a continuous string of trade-offs!

After lunch with Gustavo, they decided to freshen up and meet by the pool to decide where to go next. Sebastian arrived first so he ordered ahead. He saw Victor Mendoza waving as he approached him.

"Glad I caught you before you left." Victor sat down.

"Guess you're lucky."

"Always. I found the tape where Meyer met with Costly."

Sebastian sat up straight. "Really?"

Victor nodded. "Where's Gustavo?"

"Went to his room. He'll be here any minute."

"We can wait for him then go to my office. Okay?"

"Heck with him, I'm anxious to see it." He stood up.

Gustavo arrived just as Victor stood up.

"What's up?"

"Mendoza found the recording."

"Great. Let's go see it."

"Yeah, we were just waiting for you." Sebastian said with a straight face, but caught Mendoza smiling, so he winked at him.

Mendoza led them across the street and back to his office. This time they sat in the area used for personnel training. A small square table held a laptop connected to a multimedia projector. "I figured we'd see it better on the wall screen."

Sitting behind the computer, Mendoza worked the unit. Sebastian sat on his right and Gustavo took the left. Mendoza looked up, turned his head left, then right. "Feels crowded here!" he said and laughed.

The projector came to life, first with a blue screen, then it flickered and an image of the hotel's reception building filled the screen. However, the right edge had a glare from the daylight coming through the window. Mendoza went to close the blinds.

Black and white images appeared on the screen, where it was evening. All the lights were on, making the building look grand and elegant. The image looked pixilated, maybe because it was not intended for such a large screen, or maybe the camera was just low resolution. Sebastian had seen similar feeds before and knew the small green shape of a running man along bottom of the screen, meant it was motion-activated. The date and time appeared on the lower right corner in bold white letters. Several people milled about the reception area.

"Mister Costly is coming about ... now. There." A tall black guy entered through the center door. He looked all around then went to one of the sofas in the sitting area.

"By that time, he had been announced to our guest. He was directed to wait there."

"Yes, I remember you said nobody could enter the premises without authorization," said Sebastian.

The man in the image sat looking uncomfortable, rubbing his large hands on his knees and craning his neck each time the door opened. Then he stood and went to pour coffee in a plastic cup from the complimentary station in the center of the room.

Mendoza said, "Here comes Meyer." A man wearing dark slacks, a white short-sleeve shirt, and dark shoes appeared.

"I half expected shorts and sandals," Gustavo said.

"We now know it was a business trip for him. He's a lawyer after all. Trust me, I know the type." Sebastian could not recall Uncle Mike ever wearing jeans.

"A divorce made you acquainted with lawyers?" Mendoza asked.

Sebastian caught Gustavo's grimace. He thought the comment was out of line but Mendoza was not aware of Sebastian's widower status. That comforted him in a weird sense because it meant the news of his loss had not been spread around like party favors. The truth was that Sebastian hated pity the most.

"No, but I have some close relatives who make a living in law." Sebastian realized something else. The fact that he did not bite off Mendoza's head for innocently reminding him of the loss of his family meant something. He sighed, made a mental note to ask Dr. Jones about it. He could not believe he was looking forward to his next meeting. Damn, he needed a drink!

Focusing on the screen, they watched Meyer engaged in animated conversation with Costly.

"Shame we have no audio." Gustavo must have read his mind.

"Well, it's for security not surveillance. Mics would be invasion of privacy." Mendoza's tone bordered on self-defense.

"I guess you're right."

The conversation between the lawyer and his guest lasted long enough for Sebastian to ask Victor to fast-forward it. The video showed both men standing up, followed by Meyer walking to the desk, where he said something to the receptionist and then, together with Costly, exiting the building.

"I asked the receptionist if she remembered what Mr. Meyer said, but she can't recall."

"It's been too long. We can't really blame her," Gustavo said.

189

"Do you know where they headed?"

"I think so. Look at this." Mendoza touched a few keys, moved the mouse a couple of clicks, and the image on the screen changed. Now the vehicle entrance was visible. Sebastian thought it was from the top of the gate. A gray sedan drove up, stopping just long enough to wait for the arm to lift.

"You saw it?"

"What?" Gustavo looked at Sebastian.

"It was probably too fast. Here, let me run it again."

He pushed a few more buttons, the image froze, rewound to the point where the car was about to cross and then froze again.

"How is this?"

Sebastian could only see the car. He turned to see Gustavo who was also straining to see whatever it was that Mendoza was so excited about. "Sorry, Victor, but I can't see what you mean," Sebastian gave up.

Mendoza rolled his eyes. He stood up and walked to the screen. He pointed to a spot on the roof of the car. Something was there, on the passenger's side.

"Fingers!" Gustavo jumped up.

"Yes. There is the hand of someone riding along. It looks Caucasian. I checked the playback and Costly arrived alone."

"It could be coincidence. Maybe he met someone else here." Gustavo said. Sebastian thought that playing devil's advocate suited the Honduran.

"I don't believe in coincidences, Gustavo. Come on, do they really exist?"

The room went quiet. Sebastian considered the implications. Somehow, he knew Gustavo's thoughts would be on a similar wavelength. One person arrives, they meet, and then two leave. The angle of the camera, positioned to catch the driver only, did not allow for confirmation of the passenger's face.

That was a shame, but there was no point crying over it. It had to be Meyer, or at least, the chances were on that. That could be a safe bet.

"Okay, let's assume that, for sake of argument, they left together. Where does that lead us?"

Gustavo paced around, then approached the screen to take a better look.

"We are not looking for Meyer alone. We can search for Costly, too. *Puchica*, we can try to track the car down as well." The car's license plate was clearly visible.

"You find any of the three—" Mendoza said.

"—and you could find them all," finished Gustavo.

The exercise had broadened their search. Sebastian was not sure it would give them any advantage although searching for three needles in the proverbial haystack might be an easier feat. He had never been a gambling man but he knew enough to know most gamblers depended on percentages. The higher the probability, the higher the bet.

"What now?" Sebastian asked.

"Let's find out if the car was reported stolen. Who would do that?" Gustavo looked at Mendoza.

"Momma Costly." He meant Costly's mother. Sebastian had heard the police officer calling her that too.

"I guess no more margaritas for now," said Sebastian.

"We have three more hours of daylight. I say we go visit her."

Gustavo walked toward the door. Sebastian stood up, shook hands with Victor, and followed.

191

CHAPTER THIRTY ONE

Taking the Lada, Gustavo and Sebastian left the hotel and followed the directions they received from Inspector Perez.

Mrs. Costly lived in the area called Tornabé. To get there, they had to return to the main road and drive back a few kilometers to San Pedro Sula. Seeing a Texaco service station on the left side, Gustavo pulled over.

"Need gas," he explained.

His car had an annoying defect. Designed for low temperatures, the tank had no air intake, to prevent the gas from freezing, but in this Caribbean hot weather, that condition was a fire hazard. The 'intelligent' solution the car dealers found was to puncture the pipe, just a few centimeters below where the nozzle went in. The downside ironically, was that the tank would leak when filled up. The Solomonic solution was never to have the tank more than three-quarters full.

He got out and gave the station attendant his order.

Sebastian got out, too. "I'm going to the store. Want anything?"

"Iced tea, thank you."

He watched Sebastian walk to the store and disappear behind the door. The sun had begun to descend but even at four o'clock in the afternoon, the heat was intense. He figured he had just over two hours of light. He hoped the interview would be straightforward and quick. He did not like to drive at night.

Gustavo paid the pump attendant, waited for his receipt and stepped back in the car. After he got his slip, he turned the engine, switched on the aircon, and moved the car to park in front of the store. Soon after, Sebastian came out carrying two plastic bottles.

"Didn't know you had bottled coconut water here," he commented as he got in. He passed Gustavo his tea and took a swing at his own bottle. "This stuff's great!"

Gustavo had to smile. "Glad you like it."

They pulled onto the highway but not long after took a side road across from the station. It was a black asphalt top that seemed fresh and new. Gustavo remembered it as a dirt road back in the days he came here with his family on Sundays to spend the day at the beach. He hadn't returned since.

"Where is it we're going again?" Sebastian lowered his window so a gush of fresh air filled the car. "Do you mind going with the window down? I like the sea breeze."

In reply, Gustavo switched off the aircon. "We're going to Tornabé. It's a Garifuna town."

"Garifuna?"

"Colored people."

"Didn't take you for a racist."

"I'm not." Gustavo shrugged. "I'm just explaining the facts. The Garifuna are descendants of slaves, from a ship marooned here some 300 years ago. They settled along the Coastal area. They are very proud of their African heritage. You saw the little girls back at the hotel, right?" Sebastian nodded. "They braid your hair and sell you bread made with a coconut mix."

"Hey, Don't get so worked up. I was joking."

"Yeah, right. Anyway, we don't treat them like you guys did before the sixties. We coexisted very well. Hey, some of our best soccer players are black. Listen, they had some English influence and that's why some of their names will sound familiar to you. Plummer, Bayley,

Costly, even some first names too."

"Like Jimmy James?"

"Exactly."

"Gotcha. Gustavo, do you still think Meyer ran away?"

Gustavo took his time before answering. This new development had been unexpected. He would have understood if Costly had been a pimp, but the police had no such record of him. Small time hustler yes, but nothing more. Costly's disappearance turned the water murky. "Too early to say," he concluded.

"Damn! You should go into politics. Such diplomacy might be useful."

The main street of Tornabé was a dirt road that ran parallel with the coast, with single-story houses on both sides of the road. None had fences and all were spaced at irregular intervals. Most were painted white, a few green, but all had the typical A-frame roof.

They passed a small cemetery and a few Coca-Cola shacks, before they reached Mrs. Costly's house. Hers was white. The doors however stood out from the rest, painted a dark gray.

Gustavo parked in front. They stepped out and approached the entrance. It had a front porch where a wooden worn-out rocking chair sat next to a multicolored hammock. The main door stood open, secured against the wind by a rock in the lower corner. A screen door deterred the bugs from entering the house. Gustavo rapped on the doorframe.

"Yes?" A woman stood partially concealed behind the screen.

"Hello. My name is Gustavo Fonseca. My friend is Sebastian Martin. We'd like to talk to you about Jimmy James."

Although her profile was barely visible, Gustavo sensed her stiffening at the mention of the name.

"You with the police?"

"No, ma'am. We are with an insurance company."

"My Jimmy don't have insurance."

"We know, but we can better explain to you if we come in."

"I hear you fine from there. Explain."

She wouldn't give an inch. Gustavo wondered why. He briefed Sebastian in a few short sentences, but his contribution was limited to a tight smile.

"Ma'am, we are trying to find a missing person who had insurance."

"So you are not looking for Jimmy?"

"No, but I—"

She cut him off, "Then I have nothing to discuss with you." She moved away from the door.

Gustavo turned to Sebastian, who could not contain his laughter any longer. "Tough cookie?" he teased.

"The worst." He sighed.

They stood there for a minute, willing Mrs. Costly to change her mind. When it was obvious she wasn't coming back, they returned to the car. Gustavo placed the key in the door lock. As he turned the key, he gave the house a parting look.

The screen door opened. A young black man wearing a red-and-white stripe polo over faded jeans walked out, followed by Mrs. Costly. Gustavo saw now that she was a portly woman. The bottom of her flower-patterned long skirt swayed as she walked. She wore a loose blouse, her afro tamed under the influence of gel and some brave hairpins.

"I'll come back next week, Mrs. Costly."

"See you then, Gregorio. Say hello to your mother."

The man glanced in their direction, his gaze lingering for a moment on the car. He did not break his stride, and within a few paces, had turned the corner and was out of sight.

"Okay, what is it that you want?" She glared at them.

She stood on the edge of the porch, her hands resting on her hips, looking imposing, like a goddess or queen granting an audience.

"May we come in, please?"

"Now that you have showed some good manners, yes." She went inside, indicating for them to follow her.

Although she said it in Spanish, it seemed the meaning was not lost on Sebastian. Gustavo caught him smiling again. They entered the house and took a seat in the living room.

"Anything to drink?"

"No, thank you." Gustavo said while Sebastian shook his head.

"Like I said, we work for an insurance company. About six months ago, a man came to Honduras, stayed a few days in Telamar, then disappeared without trace."

"What does that have to do with my son? He is also missing."

"We know. The connection comes from the hotel's log for visitors. A Jimmy James Costly went there. When did your son disappear?"

"Around the same time."

"We were able to check police records that show you didn't report him missing until a short while ago."

She fidgeted, looked down at the floor, the façade melting away. "At first I thought he had gone on a drinking spree. He is a *patero*." The woman's eyes filled with tears, but it seemed she was determined not to cry in front of them.

Gustavo sympathized with her pain. His own father had also been a *patero,* an alcoholic, who could go on a binge for days or weeks. He would disappear for a few days, drink until the money ran out or the hangover caught up.

His mother said nothing, shrugged when asked about her wayward husband, and concentrated on looking

196

after her two sons. She'd cry herself to sleep, unable to get a divorce thinking she lacked the means to support the family without his income.

He remembered when he was about fifteen his mother asked him and his older brother to look for their father and gave them two hundred Lempiras for the task.

Without a clue of where to begin, the Fonseca brothers turned to their uncle. He directed them to a low-life tavern in the worst part of Tegucigalpa with cheap but strong alcohol and women who would charge for a quickie up against a wall, or on an old spring bed in a dirty room in the back.

Sure enough, they found their father there, passed out on table, his head resting in a pool of his own vomit. Gustavo remembered how the man reeked. When they tried to take him away, a large man approached them. They had to settle the bill. It seemed his father had run out of money the day before but although he could not pay, his drunken logic kept him ordering.

The boys paid the bill with the money their mother had given them and then carried their father home.

Yes, Gustavo understood. "And then?"

"When he took longer than normal, I checked his usual places." He pictured the woman walking into God knows how many forsaken joints. "In the end, I went to the police. They said they'd look for him but I don't believe them."

"What can you tell us about his mood, or what he had been doing the previous day?"

"He was happy. He said he'd found a partner to start his business."

"What business?" Gustavo remembered the police record, that Jimmy James had been a con man.

"I better show you." Mrs. Costly went into the kitchen and returned carrying three short glasses and a bottle.

197

She placed them all on the small round coffee table.

She handed the bottle to Gustavo. He looked at the label, which read 'Costly's finest Guifitti.' He gave the bottle to Sebastian who tried to read it aloud.

"Sebastian, don't look at how it is written. The name is pronounced 'gee', like in geek, 'fee' like in admission fee, and 'tee' like in golf tee."

"Guifitti." His pronunciation was close enough. "Okay, what is this stuff?"

"It's a fermented drink. Part of the garifuna's heritage. The recipe passes from father to son for generations. Very tasty, made out of roots and a bunch of other things I don't know. It's also said to have aphrodisiac properties."

Sebastian's right eyebrow arched up.

"This one was made by my son. Want to try it?" She took the bottle from Sebastian and poured two inches of the amber liquid into each glass. She passed the glasses around.

Gustavo took a short sip, prepared. He had tasted it before. He warned Sebastian not to finish it like tequila or he'd regret it.

"It's very good." Gustavo said as a courtesy; he'd never liked the bitter-sweet taste.

"I know." Her voice resonated with pride. "I taught him how to prepare it. Jimmy said he'd found a partner to start a business to commercialize it."

"Did he say the name of this partner?"

"No."

"Did you ever hear of Frank Meyer?"

She shook her head.

CHAPTER THIRTY TWO

TELA, HONDURAS

Howard Gonzales went out to light a Marlboro. He blew perfect circles of smoke as he inspected his domain. Under the pretense of a car repair shop, located down the road bordering Highland Creek, it looked the part to the last detail. It comprised a rectangular unpaved yard, fenced by a seven-foot wall with sliding wrought-iron gates at the front.

A few old car carcasses lay about in various stages of decay. Three stolen cars were parked on the right. The license plates had been changed. Another car, an old Jeep had the hood open and the engine hung from a chain on a track. They were replacing the pistons. The blue Dodge Caravan was also there. Howard was expecting to complete a fleet of five before making his next trip to Guatemala.

A shack stood at the far end, against the wall. It was nothing more than a square construction with a zinc roof, divided into two rooms, each with its own bathroom. One room was used as an office; the other held a queen-size bed with one decrepit nightstand, a dresser, a writing desk, and chair.

Another smaller shack stood against the other corner and served as a warehouse. Howard spent three nights every week there; he used different motels and women for the rest.

Marcos had taken Pablo and Miguel on a mission.

Through the window, Carlos was visible, hunched over his computer. It had been a slow week. The group made a delivery once a month, but they were running on seven weeks now, and still short. This made him edgy, which also made him smoke. He blew more rings as he fumed about his poor run.

A clang came from the front. Howard looked up. The gate parted a little and Gregorio squeezed in. He walked to where Howard stood and without preamble dropped the bomb. "We have a problem."

"What happened?" He exhaled another perfect circle of smoke.

"I was visiting Mamma Costly when—"

"How many times do I have to tell you?" Howard flicked the Marlboro butt and stomped on it with his heavy boot. "Stop visiting her!"

Gregorio looked down. Last night's downpour had turned the dark soil into pools of mud. He concentrated on a smudge on his moccasins.

Howard sighed, then said in an even voice, "This is no time to grow a conscience. It was unfortunate but we had to get rid of the problem. Visiting her puts us all in jeopardy."

"I know but—"

"But nothing! If you go there one more time, you will share her son's fate. Is that clear?" Howard's experience had proved his gaze alone could be intimidating. Gregorio shrank under it but Howard considered there must be a reason he'd brought up the point.

"What is it you wanted me to know?"

Gregorio looked up, encouraged. "Two men visited her today. They asked questions about Jimmy."

"Police?"

He shook his head. "They said they were from the insurance company."

"That can't be. Carlos checked and he had no insurance."

"They also said it wasn't about Jimmy."

A frown appeared on Howard's face. That could only mean one thing. "Anything else?"

"One looked Hondureño, and the other one was a tall gringo. They told Mamma Costly they are staying in Telamar."

"Did they arrive in a cab?"

"No, they drove there. And Boss, you're gonna love this. It was an orange Niva."

Back in Nicaragua where Howard had been born, a large number of Lada's had circulated on the streets for a long time. The Soviet influence that forbade the government from importing anything from any non-communist source, had limited the country's vehicular choice to such an extent that Ladas were pretty much all you saw there. There was a four-door sedan, a station wagon and the model Howard had liked the most, the four-wheel-drive jeep. "Is it the jeep-style?"

Pablo nodded in response.

The tips of Howard's mouth curled into a mischievous smile, tinged with longing. Howard had a design ready for it. He had actually discussed it with the boys. Probably that was the reason why Gregorio had been so eager to share his news.

Some years before as he drove back from Puerto Cortés, he had caught up with a black car. No roof, instead, a set of bars with high beams affixed to the top. It had wide tires. At first, he'd thought it was a Jeep Wrangler, but it did not have the classic taillights. The taillights looked somewhat familiar. After following the car for ten miles, he'd realized it was a Lada Niva with the top sawn off!

He had searched for one ever since, but since the nineties, they'd been almost 'extinct'. Even in Nicaragua, by the early years of the new millennium, he could not get his hands on one.

"It looked well taken care of, too," Gregorio added.

Howard envisioned what he would do with the vehicle. He looked around the garage, all the tools he needed were there: the chainsaw, acetylene tanks, even a small hoist to levitate the engine. Yes, the car would run better with a Toyota truck engine.

However, there were also practical considerations to having strangers sniffing so close to his operational base. Killing a gringo would be no easy feat in Honduras; the U.S. Embassy was very powerful and influential and they could raise hell and lean on the police. They had done so on previous occasions, when one of their citizens had been given a raw deal.

Americans looked after their own; he had to grant them that. If he was going to do this, it had to be quiet, clean, and fast. He needed Marcos.

CHAPTER THIRTY THREE

TELA, HONDURAS

The Lada accelerated on its way out of Tornabé but Gustavo's thoughts were not on the road ahead. He tried hard to figure a way to convince Mrs. Costly to give them the information about the car. She had been adamant. On the other hand, Gustavo thought knowing about the car was a lost cause. He felt they were nowhere near a solution. He did not expect to find either Jimmy James or Frank Meyer. He'd consider himself lucky if he found out where the pair went, let alone alive.

Albeit improbable, he still thought Meyer had fled. He had stolen money from his partners and Costly seemed 'connected', a person who could provide new passports. The why or how he and Meyers had found each other still nagged. He'd asked Bill Knox to check with Mrs. Meyer but she didn't know either. She had checked his two email accounts with no result, although she admitted the possibility of her husband having another email account unknown to her.

Many men did; how else would they get their porn? Anyone could open a new email account with no paper trail or credit card transaction.

Sebastian rode in silence next to him, lost in his thoughts. Neither he nor Gustavo had bothered to turn on the radio. They rode amidst the sounds of the low hum coming from the air conditioner and various engine sounds.

Gustavo reckoned he was a few miles shy of the station where he had filled up. Up ahead, he saw a blue Dodge Caravan parked on the right. The driver had stopped on the actual road, rather than pull off to the side. Jacked up at the rear, the Caravan had a bright fluorescent orange hazard triangle placed in front. Gustavo geared down and signaled his intention to change lanes to pass.

However, the tire was in place. Something else caught Gustavo's eye: the wheel had a fancy decorative hub. It was impossible to unscrew the bolts with the hub on so why was the vehicle jacked up when the tire was in place? Two men stood behind the car engaged in an animated conversation. Something was amiss. Gustavo could not tell exactly what, but his time in the army had taught him to trust his gut and at this moment, his gut clenched over something other than intestinal problems.

Keeping the left hand on the wheel, Gustavo reached with his right under the dashboard. The previous year he had installed a secret compartment there. He depressed a pin that prevented any accidental opening and a small door sprung open. He closed his hand around the A.S.P. and pulled it out.

Sebastian let out a surprised gasp, then frowned. All this took less than a second during which Gustavo had not taken his eyes off the parked car.

Gustavo was about to dismiss the feeling and blame his paranoia, when the Caravan's back door slid open. His mind registered it in slow motion. Seated inside was a third man. He held a machine gun trained on them.

Gustavo saw the flash of the muzzle before he heard the characteristic sound of an AK-47. Almost at the same time, he swerved the car to the right toward the men in the road.

With one hand on the non-hydraulic steering wheel, Gustavo maneuvered and missed hitting the Caravan by a couple of inches, only to plunge into the ditch. The car did not have air bags. Sebastian's flimsy seatbelt had no hope of restraining him and he smashed his head against the windshield. Gustavo flew forward too but did not hit it. However, the impact made him loosen his grip on the handgun, which dropped out of sight.

"Are you okay?" He turned to see Sebastian leaning forward. He pushed him back onto the seat. He was limp. Blood trickled from a nasty gash on his forehead.

Feeling dizzy, Gustavo turned his head and, through the back window, saw two men rushing to the car. He looked down searching for his gun as he thought there were three of them. Where was the third?

As if in response, he heard his door yanked open. He turned in time to see the butt of a machine gun coming at his temple and all went dark.

* * * *

Howard Gonzales saw the gate slide open. The van entered and parked to one side. The metallic scratching sounded as the gate closed again. He approached the car as Marcos got out.

"Where is my Lada?"

"I told Manuel and Gregorio to drive around for a bit. They should be here in about ten minutes."

Howard looked up at the sky at the sun rushing down. He estimated it'd be dark within thirty minutes. Meanwhile, Marcos opened the car's back door. A leg that ended with a Caterpillar walking boot dangled out. Howard leaned in for a better look.

"Who's that?"

"The gringo asking about Costly."

"He's huge, but I thought there were two."

"We separated them. No sense in having two unconscious men in a single car."

"Makes sense. Take this one out to the warehouse."

"Prepare him as usual?"

Howard frowned. It was weird Marcos would refer to it as usual. To tie a man to a chair in their stockroom was quite the opposite of usual, in fact.

In the four years they'd run the operation, this would be the second time. The first being over three years ago, when a police officer walked into the garage demanding fifty percent of their income or else he'd bust their asses.

He'd thought to sweat the cop a little before getting rid of him, wanting to establish how much the police knew or, even more important, if the cop had already ratted them out to somebody else.

He did not believe in physical pain to bring out sensitive information. People would say anything under excruciating circumstances. He knew that, as he had done his share of employing such techniques.

He was quite skilled in electric shock, waterboarding, pulling nails. Done them all. He spent most of the eighties in the service of the now defunct KGB. Taught by tough Soviets, he'd learned ways to inflict such pain.

In the good old days, his preference was to play with fire. Small doses of sharp pain proved more effective than a sledgehammer on toes. He'd found cigarette burns to be very efficient. Hell, he'd become addicted to nicotine using people's forearms as ashtrays!

Marcos and Pablo dragged the big gringo toward the warehouse. Howard raised his hand then turned to address Carlos, "Get his wallet. Learn everything you can on the man. *Rápido!*"

Carlos rushed to the side of the still unconscious man, patted him, found the wallet and left to find more information on the internet.

In the final days of the Cold War, Howard had learned that psychological pressure provided results that were even more reliable. He'd embraced his newfound techniques with gusto, but as with anything in life, it came with a downside. That particular branch of interrogation required time to deprive a prisoner of sleep and food. Time to gather the intel that could be useful. People responded better under the deceit of a loved one being tortured or dead.

This time, however, he had no such luxury. Of course he was not after national secrets, just to find out how much Mrs. Costly had babbled, if only to decide whether she needed removing too. Ugly and dirty would have to cut it this time. He spotted Pablo coming out of the warehouse and signaled him to approach.

"Get me another pack of Marlboros and matches."

CHAPTER THIRTY FOUR

TELA, HONDURAS

The pain came before consciousness. In fact, Gustavo figured the ache was what woke him. He lay on his right side with his hands tied at his back; he tried to move his feet and discovered they were bound too. He opened one eye, and after a second or two, he recognized the black leather of the backseat of the Lada. Glancing up, there was nothing but black through the window. Daylight had gone and he had no idea how long he had been out.

Gustavo knew better than to try anything at that point. He kept quiet, hoping his captors would speak, thinking him still unconscious. His gamble paid off.

The car was in motion. A stocky man sat behind the wheel. The black guy in the passenger seat looked familiar.

"Manuel, when are we going back to the garage?"

"In a while. Marcos told us to arrive later."

"Hey, watch the road!" Too late. The stocky one, named Manuel, drove straight into a pothole.

Gustavo cringed. It upset him that they were driving his car as if it were only fit for a mud rally. After a little while, he thought the driver purposely sought out the potholes. He remained down, grunting at every jolt, but keeping the appearance of still being out.

Stealing a glance, he discovered Manuel seemed a few facial hairs short of a gorilla. The other man, he remembered, was the one he'd seen coming out of Mamma Costly's house. Did she call him Gregorio?

He considered his options for taking on these two guys: being tied up was a major handicap. Also, there was no space to run and ram them. He had learned a few football moves with some American soldiers back when he served in the Army.

Resigned, Gustavo planned to play dead until they arrived at wherever the hell this garage was they had mentioned and do whatever he could when they pulled him out of the back seat. Not much more he could plan than that. He hoped it'd be the skinny one because he calculated he outweighed him by at least fifty pounds. With some luck, he might even knock him out cold. Then what? Duck under the car? If the other guy was standing near and Gustavo could move under the car fast enough, before the surprise wore off, he might be able, using both legs, to kick the guy to the ground. The guy named Manuel was bulky, so he'd fall like a rock. Then a kick to the jaw. Yes, that should do it.

Another pothole. Gustavo hung suspended in the air for a second and fell hard on his left shoulder. The sharp pain shattered his daydream.

He forced himself to think of a way out. There was always a machete in his trunk. He could access the trunk from the back seat. He shook his head. That plan was dumb considering how trussed up he was.

"Should I report now?" asked Gregorio.

"Yes. Tell them we'll get there in ten minutes. I think we've done enough circling around."

"Besides we don't have *another* spare tire."

The comment elicited a growl from Manuel, who exacted revenge with the next pothole. Gustavo felt the car accelerate, veering to the left. With the massive jolt, he almost bounced above the back of the seat. Gregorio took the hit harder, banging his head with the roof.

"Ouch!"

"Keep whining, *pendejo*."

"You're so —" but he never finished the sentence.

Gustavo did not see Gregorio's face, but he figured the man had thought better of it, or was the recipient of a killing stare from the driver. Either way, the little guy remained hushed.

The countless bumps taught Gustavo how not to land. He turned a little while in the air, so he dropped down in a better position: face down. As he came down, something lying on the floor caught his attention.

Because the Lada had only two doors, the whole front seat lifted, pivoting at the front, to give wide access to the back seat. That left plenty of room beneath the seat. A glimmer of hope, and a far more plausible plan took shape in his head.

Again, it all boiled down to his handicap. He had to have more freedom of movement; his brand-new plan depended on it. He tried to wiggle his hands out of his binding, but the outer part of his wrist started to bleed. He looked down at his feet; a plastic strap secured them. He'd seen similar devices used as disposable handcuffs. No wonder his wrists felt raw. He was rubbing against hard plastic.

He sighed and concentrated on finding something else to do. Then another bump on the road gave him an idea. He readied himself, waiting for the next one.

"Come on. Don't let that be the last one," Gustavo thought, or rather prayed.

As if on cue, a new bump gave him the room he needed. While in the air, he pushed his hands as far down as he could. He bent forward and pulled up his knees to his chin. When he landed, Gustavo pulled his hands from behind, over his feet.

He'd done it. He reached under the seat and picked up his A.S.P. In keeping with military discipline, his firearm was in Condition Two: a round chambered, safety on lock position and the hammer down.

Gustavo pointed the handgun at the nape of Gregorio's neck and cocked the hammer. As he had anticipated, the distinctive metallic sound of a firearm drew gasps from the pair in front.

The gorilla lookalike turned his head in the direction of the sound. "What the—"

"Shut up! Don't look back and keep driving!" Gustavo said.

"I searched you. You had nothing!" the black guy said, a look of confusion plain on his face.

"Ask and you shall receive. Don't you have faith in miracles? Now, where're we heading?"

"To Highland—"

"Don't tell him!" yelled Manuel.

Too late, Gustavo knew about the place called Highland Creek. It was on the way out of Tela toward La Ceiba. The road was smooth now, so he figured they had reached the main road. "Hey, I can read the sign now. We're almost there. Make your turn."

Manuel made a sound akin to a dog growling but turned left at the sign. Now they were on a dirt road again. It ran along the river that gave the name to the place. They continued for a while.

The radio was off and an eerie silence filled the inside of the car. Gustavo was at a stalemate, not sure how to continue. He did not know how many others were at the place. He thought about going back, calling for reinforcements, and raiding the place. While making his plans, he kept the A.S.P. muzzle trained on Gregorio's nape.

The driver stamped on the brakes and veered to the right. The car sped off the road and down a steep path, then crashed into the river. From the corner of one eye, Gustavo caught an arm flying his way, but too late. The elbow connected with his face. White patches clouded his vision.

He blinked several times. He shook his head. The patches still showed. Disoriented, he sensed rather than saw Gregorio turning to face him from behind the white areas. A hand holding a gun came into view. He did not know who it was. His instinct told him it must be Gregorio.

He let his military training take over and pulled the trigger in his assailant's general direction, but he saw the flash of another muzzle. The shots reverberated in the closed compartment. Even with the poor aim, Gustavo's bullet found a target in the upper right corner of Gregorio's forehead. His body lay inert on the seat. However, the other bullet did some damage as Gustavo felt a zing in his upper arm as though he'd been branded with a hot iron.

The smell of gunpowder filled Gustavo's nostrils, but he had little time to think about that, or the fire in his arm. Manuel's reaction was quick, but inefficient because he could not fully turn around. Still, he twisted his torso beyond where Gustavo would have thought possible. The thick Popeye-like forearm pushed his hands away, followed by an iron grip that would not let him pull the trigger again. Gustavo's position even if advantageous, was limited by his bound hands; the powerful grip took its toll and Gustavo dropped the gun.

Manuel attempted to elbow him again. This time Gustavo was ready, blurred vision and all, and ducked out of its merciless path. With his bound hands, he made an upward ark, stopping Manuel's hand. Manual's hand, however, took a grip on Gustavo's neck. He tried to punch down but it felt like hitting a brick wall. He gagged, his lungs on fire. He thought it would be his end, strangled by a gorilla.

His vision dimmed. He looked down, past the killing

arm, to the floor. He did not see his gun, not that he could reach it anyway. With one last effort, Gustavo changed position, slid down from the seat to the car's floorboard. Manuel stretched, his determined grip still in place, but the position was more uncomfortable and the grip slackened. Gustavo pushed the other man's hand away as he twisted face down. The sound of fabric against the leather seat told Gustavo Manuel was coming after him.

Gustavo was quick to find his salvation. Knowing every inch of his car gave him the advantage. He took the handgun, flipped over and fired at point blank range. The blast deafened him, but luck stayed with him and the second bullet found its mark too.

The projectile hit the man in the arm, but he was still conscious. Gustavo punched the shoulder, which brought a loud wail. Manuel, not beaten yet, lunged at Gustavo with his free arm. The blow connected, this time a full fist square in the face. Gustavo tasted blood and something hard, presumably a tooth, and saw Manuel raise his arm. The next blow would render him unconscious. He fired. Manuel's bloody face slid down, out of view.

Gustavo's breathing came in short bursts, hyperventilating. He felt cold. He moved his feet and felt his shoes soaked. The river was coming into the car, rising at a steady and icy rate. He placed the gun on the seat where it would stay dry. He knelt and looked behind the seat, into the trunk, and found what he was looking for.

He placed the nine-inch machete between his thighs, moving the cuffs against its blade. With free hands, he cut his feet loose. He grabbed the gun and tried to open the door. The water pressure from outside was too strong so he climbed out through the open window.

The river ran knee-deep. He looked up at the ford, expecting to see curious onlookers but he found the place deserted. He walked toward the edge and sat on the dry soil to catch his breath.

His face hurt. He'd had similar close encounters in the past and survived, scarred but alive. He put the firearm in his belt, and then washed his face. The cold river water revived him enough to remember he had not begun this journey alone.

CHAPTER THIRTY FIVE

TELA, HONDURAS

Sebastian had developed a nose for flammable liquids such as gasoline or diesel. He assumed it came with the territory, as one who fought against the hell such liquids could create. Now, in this darkened room, he sniffed something he could not identify.

He faced the back wall, a small window placed high. The glass looked coated with grease. Right under the window was a large poster of a woman wearing a thong and a lascivious smile, as if inviting him. A calendar from the previous year hung underneath.

He looked around and saw wood shelves with different kinds of tools. He recognized some of them and deduced he must be in a garage or workshop. That accounted for the odor he could not distinguish: it was the long time mixture of gasoline, grease, oil, and God only knows what else.

He sat on a wood chair, his shirt torn off, his arms strapped to the armrest, his legs tied up as well. His head throbbed. He passed his tongue around his lips and tasted dried blood. He felt dizzy, but somehow he knew the worst was yet to come.

The sound of a door opening came from behind him, followed by the smell of smoke. Cigarettes and flammable fluids – never a good combination. Heavy steps approached from the door, then circled him.

A man wearing large reflective sunglasses stood beside

him. In one hand, he held a cigarette butt, and a handkerchief on the other. The man's skin was dark, a local. He wore khaki cargo pants and the black polo shirt seemed to blend with the poor light, giving the impression of a hovering head standing over him.

"I will make this easy for you, Gringo." The heavy accent told no tales about his mother tongue. "Just tell me what I need to know."

Sebastian looked up with a frown. He had no idea what he could possible know that would interest big sunglasses. As if in response, the man did something strange. Extending his arm, he squeezed the handkerchief until a drop of clear liquid fell on Sebastian's arm. It itched on contact, but that wasn't the end of it. The man put the lighted tip of the cigarette in the exact spot. A blue flame flared, burning the hair. The pain was sharp and intense.

Sebastian did his utmost not to scream. He looked at his right arm. An irregular circle formed, the skin raw. He recognized it as a first-degree burn, but he hadn't known it would cause such pain. However, the sharpness passed as swiftly as it had begun, leaving a sting in its wake. He looked up to the man. Sebastian figured the rag must be soaked in gas or rubbing alcohol. Damn, it hurt!

"That should give me your full attention." Big Glasses repeated the process and, if possible, it hurt more.

"What the hell do you want?" Sebastian spoke through clenched teeth.

"You know, Gringo. I used to do this for a living, trained by the best – your own CIA. Can you believe that?"

Sebastian remained quiet. He wondered if his own countrymen would teach somebody how to torture human beings. He was not naïve. He knew it must be true, but never expected to come this close to such

216

techniques.

"Man, I miss the Cold War. Back in the eighties, we had no limitations. Your President Reagan spared no expense." The man laughed a sinister laugh. "We had a limitless budget. And the training sessions? Everybody looked forward to the end of the course. There was booze, broads, the works.

"Our primary target was to keep the commie bastards at bay! We excelled at that. We captured, we tortured, we created panic in their ranks, until they had nowhere to go but back to Russia. Then, when the elections in Nicaragua finalized the return to democracy, the flow of money stopped and we had an army with no cause. So we each found our own line of business."

Another drop, another ignition. This time on his left arm. He sniffed something akin to pork skin burning. Sebastian's heart pumped hard against his chest. He did not know where this *conversation* was going. The man kept rambling about the good ole days against the Red aggression.

"You want answers? Then ask the damn questions!" he blurted out.

"No, not yet."

The man put out the cigarette on his arm. It hurt like hell, but he remained quiet. Then the man exited the room without asking anything. What the hell was he playing at?

* * * *

Howard walked into the room where Carlos hunched over his desktop. The computer printer buzzed, spitting out pages; he loved this new equipment. He remembered the old noisy dot-matrix printers that could be heard from across a crowded room.

"I have some info on the guy," Carlos said.

"I can see that." He pointed to the printer. "I don't have time to sit and read through it. Give me the highlights."

Carlos turned from his computer to face his boss, took one of the papers coming out of the printer. "He's six foot two, two hundred twenty pounds, muscular build."

"Carlos! I can learn all that just by looking at him, you idiot!"

Clearing his throat, Carlos continued reading, careful to skip the mundane bits of information. "He was born in New York, April 8. Grew up there. Joined the New York Fire Department, worked there for over ten years. Last rank he held was lieutenant and last commission was investigating arson. Has not been on active duty for the past few months."

"Why?"

"His wife and only child died in an air accident. He dropped out from the grid for about seven months. It looks as though he's trying out a new job with an insurance company in Dallas."

"Some career change."

He had started a quick mind game telling the gringo Americans had trained him, instead of Soviets. The idea was to have the subject lose hope of a rescue. If the government that was supposed to look after him gave his enemy the tools to conquer him, then why would they come charging to the rescue? Well, that was the idea anyway.

Not every subject bought it, but in the short time he had now, playing fast and dirty was the only option. Howard sat to ponder on this new information. How he could use it. Now he needed to weave in this new data, but how best to do it?

* * * *

For Sebastian, the worst part was seeing how the dark circles covered his white-skinned forearms.

"How was your visit today?" The soothing voice followed by a drop and a burn.

"What the hell do you want?" What kind of mind trick was this, to apply pain but ask stupid questions?

"Nothing much. Only the truth." A drop. A burn.

The only person he had visited that day was the old lady. Still, somehow he felt certain his captor already knew that, even if not admitting to it.

"You have massive forearms, like a sailor. I'm about to draw an anchor. You will look like Popeye." Another drop. Another burn.

It hurt every time.

He looked down. Big Glasses had lied. There was nothing shaped like anchors on either of his arms, only the dark circles that now occupied almost every inch of his arm. How long had he been there?

"I know about Kelly and Joshua." The man said and Sebastian looked up to his captor. "I knew that would get your attention." A drop. A burn.

"What do you care about them?"

"I really couldn't care less about your dead family, but I wanted you to know that I know." A drop. A burn.

"Damn it! Then what the fuck do you want?" he said through clenched teeth.

The man smiled. "Now we're making progress." Another drop. Another burn.

"You're twisted. You torture me but don't ask me any meaningful questions. Are you doing it just for the fun of it?"

Big Glasses stood, took a step back, a permanent smile on his face. "I'll be back in five minutes. I ran out of gas." He squeezed the rag to show no more liquid came out of it. Then he left.

* * * *

Howard Gonzales walked into the office. Marcos sat on the couch, a beer can in his hand. Carlos, as usual, hunched over his computer.

"How is it going?"

"I think it is going well, Marcos. All things considered. It's hard to play mind tricks in a short time." He pulled a chair and sat next to Carlos.

"That's why you only burn him and not ask any questions?" Carlos's disgust showed on his face.

"Yes, I want him to tell me on his own, without being asked. Tricky, but it's very effective when done the right way."

"Good luck with that." Marcos raised his beer in mock toast before he drank.

"Have Manuel and Gregorio arrived?"

"Not yet."

He checked his watch. "They're late."

"You know Manuel. They probably stopped to eat."

He felt blood rush to his head. Was Marcos stupid? "And you sit there enjoying a beer while your men stop to eat with a man tied in the back seat of a bullet-riddled car?"

Marcos's reaction was abrupt and angry. He stood up, his jaw set, a deep frown creasing his forehead. He crushed the can, tossed it into a bin, and strode out while fishing a cellular phone out of his pocket.

Howard did not like surprises. Despite Marcos's remark, it wasn't Manuel's nature to stop for a meal before finishing a job. He'd better hurry things up with the tall gringo.

CHAPTER THIRTY SIX

TELA, HONDURAS

The full moon lit the dirty road for Gustavo. He had cleaned his wound and applied a combat bandage made from his shirt. Armed with his A.S.P. and machete, he moved, stealthily and fast, along the road.

He did not know this part of town. The road looked deserted, running along the river path, the water on the right and no houses on the other side. After some thirty minutes, he arrived at an eight-foot-tall perimeter fence. It was the only construction within a mile. He walked around it and estimated its dimensions to be half a city block, maybe a bit less than that. The only break in the wall was a wrought-iron gate on the side, facing the road. No back gate.

He noticed that for five feet around the fence, all the vegetation was very low. After that, the thick foliage looked impregnable. A real fortress of solitude, he noted.

The dirt road continued farther down, but his gut told him this was the place he was looking for. He needed to make sure, though. He had to find a way to peek inside.

He crossed the road to the riverbed. The water ran a tranquil route around the low bends, with a gentle babbling over the rocks. He looked around, studying every aspect and opportunity. Something caught his attention across the stream, providing him with the seed of an invasion plan.

Wary, he stepped into the creek. His shoes sank in the mud and the cold water made him gasp; his pants soaked in seconds. The current seemed manageable. He raised his gun high and took another step.

Step by careful step, with the water reaching to his knees, he crossed the creek to the other side where an old timber trunk had fallen.

After securing his A.S.P. in his waistband, he worked with the machete to hack away a thick branch. It took him a good few minutes, sweat poured down his face but he kept hacking until he severed it. The branch was just shy of four inches in diameter and almost six feet long.

He carried the branch back across the river, retracing his steps to the fence and dropped it in the farthest corner from the road. Even in the dead of night, he did not want to risk being seen from the road. Right next to the wall, he used the machete to dig out two small but deep holes spread about a foot apart. He then chopped the bough into two separate pieces of different lengths.

He planted the first one, leaning the branch against the wall for support. It stood about a foot and a half from the ground. The remaining part was twice as long and he planted it in the same manner.

Gustavo took a step back to admire his work. He now had a rough two-step ladder to reach the top of the fence. All of his labor took the best part of an hour. Now it was time to put his contraption to good use.

* * * *

Sebastian heard the door closing, followed by a couple of footsteps, then a scraping sound. His captor came from behind pulling a chair that he placed backward. The man sat down resting his arms on the back rail of the chair. Sebastian observed the hands held neither rag nor cigarette on this visit. The dark glasses were gone, too.

"Where is Gustavo Fonseca?"

"Why are you asking me? Ask the men who attacked

us." Was this a new game?

"They were supposed to arrive thirty minutes ago. No more games, now. I don't have time."

Sebastian thought about this. Big Glasses had burned circles all over his arm while talking bullshit and reminiscing about the Cold War. All of a sudden, this torturer comes empty-handed and asks about Fonseca. Was it a ruse? Or had Gustavo eluded them? If the latter were true then help would be coming. He dared not hope for it.

The door creaked open again. The man looked over Sebastian's shoulder, nodded, extended his hand to reach for whatever they were giving him. Sebastian feared it'd be the rag again. The man accepted a foot-long iron rod; a circular object affixed to the tip. He distinguished a coin, a U.S. quarter.

"The circles will be bigger now." The man smiled, looked down at Sebastian's arms, and made a sad face. "No more room on your arms. I guess we'll have to use that broad chest."

"What the hell do you want from me?" he screamed. He'd grown tired of this game.

"I told you already." The man stood up, kicked back the chair, then placed the tip close to Sebastian's face. The image blurred around the edges of the tip, as the vapor emanated from the heated rod. He looked up to his captor's eye and found deadly seriousness there.

"Would you like to see a preview?" Not waiting for a reply, the man put out his left fist. There, a little above the thumb joint, Sebastian saw the perfect circle, a spread-wing eagle, and the legend, "In God We Trust."

Sebastian's eyes widened in horror. Something else caught his eye. The man wore a silver timepiece. Sebastian frowned. The watch sparkled against the overhead light. No more than a few inches from his face, he could distinguish the letters "Oyster Perpetual." A Rolex.

He remembered that back at a gas station before leaving San Pedro Sula, a boy had approached their car to offer them counterfeit Rolexes. They were the Submariner style, not like this fancy one. He had read about a similar watch. Little bits of info floating in the ether fell into place as it all became clear. He realized what his ordeal was all about and looked up at the torturer.

Unable to restrain himself, he said, "Did you kill Frank Meyer to steal his watch?"

The man's eyes registered surprise, but he reacted with alacrity and moved his hand.

"So, you do know a bit too much for your own health. Pity." He took the rod and pushed it against Sebastian's chest.

A hissing sound, then the smell of burnt flesh filled Sebastian's nostrils before his brain processed the information. The pain came last.

* * * *

They could not be expecting an assault, Gustavo kept telling himself. One man against at least three made for difficult odds without the element of surprise. He surveyed the area inside the wall. Dirt floor, a couple of car engines, then a minivan parked at the far end. He could not be certain of the color, but minivans were uncommon in Honduras. Besides, he did not believe in coincidences. Other cars occupied the rest of the space, a large Toyota Prado, a Nissan sedan, and a Tundra pick-up truck. No local garage would be complete without an old carcass. This one had a Jeep Wrangler.

Two single story huts stood at the back of the lot. The one to the right sported a somewhat better finish. He assumed it doubled as living quarters or office space, while the other most likely served as a storage area.

From where he stood he saw the windows on this side showed no light from inside the huts. He needed more information, so he decided to look from other points.

Repositioning the makeshift ladder – he didn't dig the holes too deep this time – he spied on the right side of the lot.

From his new vantage point, he distinguished the hut had a cement porch in the front. A man wearing dark jeans with an un-tucked short-sleeved shirt over them smoked and walked about. Barrel-chested, with thick extremities, he had the appearance of a tough, weather-beaten man. Gustavo surmised he could not win in a fair fight with him.

The door opened and another man came out. Gustavo watched but could not make out any of what they were discussing. The stance made him think the newcomer was a superior. Then a final proof of who was boss: the first man fished out a cigarette, offered it and lit it while inclining his head.

After flicking the butt, the second man went back in. Gustavo strained to catch a glimpse as the door opened. He saw a third man, this one thinner, working on a computer.

Three confirmed against one, plus the unknown inside the other hut.

"Damn it." He got down. A quick look through the Lexan grip and he knew he had four bullets and no spare magazine. He sighed in frustration.

He considered his options for the tenth time. Going for help would be too late for Sebastian because of the distance and timing. His gut kept telling him the gringo was in there somewhere, and in danger. Would the gringo be alive? He feared the worst but he could not back down.

He secured the handgun inside his waistband and moved the logs a few feet to the left. He climbed up, out of sight from the housing. A narrow dirt passageway ran between the hut and fence.

He threw the machete. It flew straight down and secured itself, blade down, into the dirt floor with a soft thud. With his hand pressing hard against the edge, he pulled himself up and over the fence, then dropped. Not as quietly as the machete. He heard the loud thump, reacted by rolling to his side and pulling his gun, aiming at the empty air. He held his breath and counted to twenty.

When nobody showed up, he stood, retrieved the machete, and pressed his back against the hut's wall. Sliding sideways, he circled the house, then peeked before crossing the narrow corridor between the two constructions. He continued, slower on this side, as he knew there were men on the far side of the wall. Gustavo fought to control his heart rate with measured intakes through his nose, exhaling by mouth. He forced his mind to focus on the job at hand, to stop wondering about the "what if." The time for second-guessing had passed. Ahead lay a new tour of the battlefield.

He turned the last corner, and he knew combat awaited him just a few feet away. When he reached the edge, he slid down and popped his head around the corner for a fraction of a second, absorbing as much as possible.

His nostrils filled with cigarette smoke. Man, he was so damn close! Akin to a chess player, he mapped the next three moves in his head. The first move would be the most dangerous, the most difficult, and the most treacherous.

With a fleeting sense of regret, Gustavo jumped on the man from behind and placed his right hand over the man's mouth while severing his throat with the machete. So easily, he was a killer once again. A cold-blooded, backstabbing bastard. He recalled how he and Sebastian were ambushed, shot at, tied down, and kidnapped. He told himself the killing this time was self-defense.

He dragged the corpse to hide it around the corner. Gustavo performed a quick pat down, but found no guns. Time to change weapons. He took the machete with his left hand, flipping it to hide the blade behind his forearm. His right hand closed around the A.S.P., where the handgun felt like a natural extension of his arm. His training kicked in, in particular the part about not getting over-confident or cocky.

He had seen which way the door opened. Nothing like firsthand intel. Gustavo held his breath and kicked in the door, the surprise evident on his prey. He had prioritized his targets: he aimed at the man who had gone out to smoke.

Two shots in the chest and he dropped. He turned to face the man at the computer, who by then had jolted upward with his hands up and eyes wide, and turned white as a ghost.

Gustavo had decided before he walked in, no time for mercy. He aimed at the knee and shot once. The young man screamed, and then dropped to the floor.

"Where is the gringo?"

The computer guy did not respond, but kept wailing. Gustavo took a step forward and kicked the man's knee.

"I won't ask again."

Computer guy looked up with puffy red eyes and un-able to say a word, still managed to signal with a nod of his head toward the other hut.

"Is there anyone else?"

The guy did not respond. Gustavo flexed his knee as if to kick again. The sudden move made the kid recoil and wail, but at the same time, he shook his head.

CHAPTER THIRTY SEVEN

TELA, HONDURAS

Sebastian could still smell his own burning flesh. He felt lightheaded. A gunshot caught his attention. He shook the dizziness from his head and focused.

His gaze followed his captor around the room. The frown on his face and the frantic moves felt too elaborate to be part of a truth-extracting ruse. Sebastian remembered Gustavo and his see-through gun. He struggled to keep his hope in check.

The man climbed the shelves, peered through the dirty window, and dropped back down. He paced around like a caged lion. Sebastian followed as much as his neck would allow. The man stopped right in front of him. He moved to the chair and with a grunt-emitting effort, pivoted it on its rear legs. Sebastian now faced the door. He'd just become a human shield.

"Stay put, Gringo." He felt the man's warm breath on the back of his neck. His right arm propped the gun pointing at the entrance.

If Gustavo entered in that instant, he'd be a sitting duck. He had to do something to warn Gustavo. His captor seemed to read his mind and covered his mouth.

A metallic click and a gentle rattle came from the doorknob, as if checking to see if the door was locked. Sebastian held his breath.

The knob turned and the door opened halfway. Sebastian recognized the gait before the actual face appeared.

He bit down hard on the hand that covered his mouth until it jerked away. He yelled a single word. "Gun!"

A thunderous boom followed the flash of light on his right. Gustavo's face, in full view now, his eyes wide with surprise. Blood splattered out of his shoulder and Sebastian watched him drop to the floor.

The feeling of impotence stung worse than the burns. He had to do something. Anything. He tipped up on his toes and tilted back. It felt like slow motion, but Sebastian knew it was fast enough to prevent the man from reacting. He fell on top of him. The chair collapsed under the strain of his two hundred pounds plus, and yanking his hands free, he pounded the armed man who screamed in pain.

With his newfound freedom, he rolled to the side. The man still had the gun, and now turned it toward Sebastian. Sebastian jumped on top of him, wrapping both hands around the firearm. In the struggle, Sebastian pushed his thick finger behind the trigger so the man could not fire. They pulled left and right, and rolled together on the floor. The man brought his knee up to connect with Sebastian's crotch. He grunted in pain, the instant of distraction all that the torturer needed.

The man wiggled himself free from under Sebastian, yanked Sebastian's finger from the trigger, and aimed the gun at Sebastian's temple. Sebastian recovered his wits and connected an elbow to his assailant's eye. Then he dove for the gun again, only this time a fraction of a second too late. The shot hissed past his ear. From this new angle, he let his weight force the man's arm down to his chest, moving the aim away from himself and onto his enemy.

The man's free hand grabbed a chunk of hair and pulled. Sebastian screamed again and had the fleeting notion he was getting the worst of the fight. He closed his fist and connected a heavy punch to the side of his oppo-

229

nent's head. The guy's eyes went out of focus as a shot resounded.

Sebastian felt warm liquid against his chest, but no pain. He figured he was in shock. The man's grip on his hair loosened, and his breathing became labored. Sebastian rose up, looked down, and saw the pool of blood on the man's shirt. He noticed a small circular hole in the chest, and the blood pumping out. One last gasp and the man stopped breathing altogether. Sebastian sat, catching his breath, exhaustion taking over.

He looked at the body lying near the door. He turned Gustavo over to face him. He noticed Gustavo was shirtless and sported a bandage around his left shoulder. Blood oozed from the other shoulder now, but this time he'd been hit closer to the neck.

"We look like a gay couple laying here with our bare chests," Gustavo said with effort, then he coughed blood.

Sebastian smiled and said, "I guess so."

"That *pendejo hijueputa* lied to me."

"Who?"

"A nerd in the other hut told me nobody was here but you."

"We need to call for help."

"Check the guy's pocket. Maybe he's got a cell phone."

Sebastian helped Gustavo sit up, his back against the doorframe, and he returned to the dead body. He felt the area around the pants pockets and fished out a phone. An iPhone, no less. The guy liked to live in style.

"It's not the same as in the U.S. Dial one-nine-nine for emergencies."

"Will they speak English?"

"Pass me the phone."

He handed the phone to Gustavo and watched as he made the call.

EPILOGUE

NEW YORK, USA

Sebastian and Roger Simmons were outside an apartment in Upper West Side, Manhattan. Roger pushed the doorbell. They stood sharing the silence. Roger had called him two days earlier asking if he'd like to come. He'd accepted at once.

Sebastian thanked the cold weather that allowed him to wear long sleeves and jackets to cover his bandaged forearms. The doctors said the cigarette burns would not leave any permanent damage. The small circles had not yet healed, but were on the way. When he asked if hair would grow back on his arm doctors couldn't give him a straight answer – they did not know. Sebastian had some experience with skin burns from his time as a fireman. He knew he might walk the rest of his days with bald circular patches in his arms. At least he was alive to tell the tale. That sufficed.

Joanne Meyer opened the door. Her knee-length black skirt and white silk blouse gave her a professional appeal. She wore light makeup and stood straight, like a portrait of an aristocratic lady.

"Mr. Simmons?" she said with a deep throaty voice.

"Yes. Thank you for seeing us." He shook her hand. "This is Sebastian Martin, the man I told you about."

"Oh yes." She turned to face him and extended her hand. "I can't thank you enough for what you did. Please come in."

She led them to the living room and while Roger and Mrs. Meyer exchanged a few pleasantries, Sebastian took in the décor. The designer brown leather sofas seemed more fitting for a bachelor's pad. The minimalist coffee and lamp tables, too. The Persian carpet and the flower-shaped lamp gave an elegant balance to it all. Actual paintings hung on the wall rather than framed paper reproductions. Perhaps not Picasso or Monet, not that he could tell the difference, but the color palettes toned with the rest of the furniture. He remembered how Kelly taught him to observe the living room details whenever he visited a house for the first time. She used to say you could learn a lot from the image the owners tried to convey. Then she'd added that a glimpse of the kitchen would confirm whether it was a façade or the real thing.

"I understand you spent some time in the hospital," she said to Sebastian.

"Can't figure it out. I survived many years in the Fire Department without a scratch and then I get burnt in my first job in the insurance business."

"Insurance people live on the odds," Roger said with an apologetic smile.

"And how is your partner? I heard he was shot."

"He bitches so much you wouldn't believe he's a macho man."

"I was a registered nurse before I was married, Mr. Martin. I can assure you, a gunshot wound is no laughing matter." Mrs. Meyer looked at him with a gaze that made him shiver.

"I only joke about it because he lived through it."

"I'm sorry, the issue is still very sensitive for me."

It had been many years since he'd blushed. Now he felt angry with himself. When he'd been a fireman, he'd received training on how to break bad news to people.

"Mrs. Meyer," Roger said after clearing his throat, "Gustavo Fonseca saved Sebastian's life, and was shot in the process. Twice. But he is recovering in full. Sebastian went through his own ordeal. I believe these private hells created a bond between the men, much like the rapport seen among soldiers who were in combat together. I'm not surprised at how they treat each other."

"Maybe you're right, Mr. Simmons." The smile on her face indicated no hard feelings.

Roger pulled out an envelope from his jacket. "The reason I insisted on coming was to bring you this."

The widow took the envelope, opened it, and scanned the contents. She sighed and a tear escaped and rolled down her cheek. Sebastian wondered if her reaction was because of to the amount.

As if reading his mind, she lifted her head, her gaze fixed on him. "You must think me mad." She wiped away the tear with her hand. "It's been months and months of not knowing what happened to Frank. This check feels like a final confirmation that I will never see my husband again."

"Believe me, I know what you're going through," he said.

"How could you?"

"Sebastian is a widower," Roger said while looking at Sebastian.

"Oh, I am sorry to hear that. I ... I am sorry I was so harsh on you."

"Don't worry. Everybody deals with pain in his own way. Mine was alcohol, but now I'm relying more on cynicism. I shouldn't have made that comment after knowing you for just five minutes."

"How did she ...?" she seemed unable to say the word aloud.

"Air crash. Last year. She and my son died."

"How horrible! Frank and I were never blessed with children."

He shrugged. The topic became uncomfortable very

fast. She must have thought the same, for she asked Roger about the amount on the check.

"We were required to deduct a large amount because of the embargo made by Mr. Meyer's former employer to recoup the sum he took from them."

"I know about that. I'm surprised because I didn't expect this much would be left."

"When the police searched the garage where they held Sebastian, they found, among other things, three stolen cars. With the discovery of Mr. Meyer's body and the confirmation that his death was not of natural causes, the company honored the policy and made out the check to cover double indemnity."

"I can't condone what he did but I'm sure my husband intended to pay that money back."

"While in Honduras," he motioned toward Sebastian, "they discovered many things, including your husband's intention to start a business. We all make mistakes and your husband was caught at the wrong place at the wrong time before he was able to put right his wrongdoing."

"Thank you. That's very kind of you."

"Mrs. Meyer." She turned to face Sebastian. "You know we could have mailed the check, but Roger insisted we deliver it in person. He invited me to come, and I agreed because I have something else to give you."

He pulled a handkerchief out of his pocket. It was heavy and contained the reason for his visit. He handed it to Mrs. Meyer, who looked puzzled. She unfolded the handkerchief and gasped at the sight of the silver Rolex.

She inspected it, turned it, and read the inscription aloud, "To Frank with love." Her eyes watered.

"Believe me, the shock it gave the man torturing me, when I challenged him about the watch, saved my life."

She dropped the high society act and cried. "I bought him this for our fifteenth anniversary."

"Some gift."

"It doubled as a private joke." She sniffed. "You see, he wanted to buy a boat, so I gave him this Rolex Yacht Master. The card said it was up to him to get the yacht." She smiled, savoring the memory.

"He planned to start a business so I guess the yacht would have come later." Roger said.

"Yes, probably." She looked straight at Sebastian, "Thank you for this. It means a lot, and I don't mean for its monetary value."

"I know what you mean."

"May I ask you a personal question?"

That caught him by surprise, but he could not think of a way to deny her. "Sure."

"My therapist swears that, with time, I will be open to meeting somebody else."

"Fire him."

"I agree with you. I think of Frank every day."

"There's not a day goes by that I don't think of Kelly and Joshua. I took a different path though."

"How so?"

"I tried to drown my pain in vodka."

"Did that help you forget?" She tilted her head.

"No, but the headache the next morning put them out of my mind, at least until the first aspirin."

"Are you still following that path?"

"No. This man," he rested his hand on Roger's shoulder, "gave me a job. Having something to do helped more."

"Better than therapy, right?"

"Yep, it kills my brother." She looked puzzled, so he explained. "He's a therapist."

She smiled. "They mean well, I'm sure. Their firm belief is that life goes on and we should move along with it."

"Yeah. My first therapist suggested I go on a date."

"Like that was easy! What did you do?"

"Fired the bastard. Even my brother got angry at him."

"I don't see myself dating." Joanne Meyer asked.

"No, I don't either," he said fast. Too fast. He noticed Roger's face and wondered what that frown could mean.

* * * *

Sebastian looked at a framed picture of himself with his dead family. He sighed, touched the faces of Kelly and Joshua with the tips of his fingers. He ached, longing to feel their warm skin. Instead, he felt the cold glass.

He put the frame inside the box on the floor. He did the same with each picture, with each memory. He would not forget his family but he needed to move on. He understood that now. Heck, even his shrink, the ever-formal Doctor Jones, was excited.

"Sebastian, you should wrap those in paper," a female voice called.

He turned to see his sister-in-law. "What?"

"If you don't wrap them you'd better use gloves opening that box."

"I ... um ..."

"Here, let me do it." Christine disappeared behind the door, returning with a bundle of old newspapers. She sat on the floor and took all the pictures out of the box. She picked up one and carefully wrapped it in a sheet of newspaper.

"This is the first time I have something else to move other than my clothes."

She smiled. "I know. Just a couple of months before your wedding. Right?" He nodded. "James and I moved a few times. We know the drill."

He looked at her, squatting on the rug while wrapping the frames with uncanny precision. It was obvious she'd done this before. It brought a smile. Kelly had never been so proficient at housekeeping. He wondered if that diametric difference was the reason why Kelly and Christine never got along. But that was past now. "Thank you."

"It's okay. We're glad you decided to take a chance in Dallas."

"I don't mean for helping me with the move." He watched as she stopped to look up at him. "I mean for everything else. You're not responsible for looking after me but I am glad that you do."

"Oh, Sebastian, don't be silly." Still, her eyes turned misty. "I should be asking you to forgive me. I know I gave Kelly a hard time. I just ..." She could not find the words.

"She was perfect for me. You just never agreed with that."

She sniffed. "Maybe not before, but now I see that she was. I'm sorry it's too late."

He put his hand on her shoulder to comfort her. "I know."

She wiped away the tears and resumed wrapping. "We'd better finish this or you'll never go."

James popped his head from behind the door. "What's up?"

Christine turned her back to her husband. "Nothing. Just sharing a memory or two." Her voice firmer when she said, "Now go finish with the closets."

Sebastian followed James to the master bedroom.

"I finished putting all Joshua's clothes in a box. Those go to the church, right?"

"Yes, also Kelly's."

"Yeah, Christine took care of that. You're the one left to sort. I don't love you enough to dive elbow-deep into your underwear."

Sebastian laughed. "It's all clean, you moron." James had always been squeamish.

"Nope, not buying it. I don't think you stopped

drinking long enough to take care of your laundry."

"I don't drink anymore," Sebastian said, his tone very serious.

He had been walking a step behind James and after hearing him, his brother stopped and turned.

"I'm sorry. I didn't mean to say that."

They were same height, their eyes level. James had piercing green eyes he hid behind thick professor-like glasses. Still, he looked sincere.

"I wonder how you can still practice psychology if you keep blundering like that with your patients." He delivered his line with a smile, intended to convey it was okay.

"You're not my patient."

"Thank God for that!" he retorted.

"You're right. I might have strangled you before now!"

"And we don't want that. Come on, let's finish this. I can't stand the two of you crying for me."

"I'm not crying. I'm merely making a point." James frowned. "Wait a minute. Who else was crying? Christine?"

"Man, you're not very intuitive, are you? No wonder she wears the pants in the house."

"She doesn't wear the pants in the house." His voice was so loud that she heard him across the hall.

"What was that, honey?" Christine called from the other room.

"Nothing, dear." He looked furious; even more so when he saw Sebastian's smile. "Shut it, or I'm sending *you* in a box."

When Sebastian finished with his clothes, his phone rang. "Hi, Uncle Mike." He guessed what this conversation would be about and he didn't want James or Christine to know about it yet. He made sure he was out of earshot.

"Hi, Seb. I just received the new offer from the airline."

"New offer?" He perked up. "What did you do? I told you to settle it."

"Oh, come on. They were offering peanuts. Do you know how much their annual cash flow alone is?"

"No, but I bet that you do. Listen, I don't want to break them. The last thing I want on my conscience is having them to layoff lots of people on my account." He was upset. He wanted closure, not a long trial with the airline trying to prove it was not their fault his family had died.

"Don't sweat it. I didn't shoot for the stars."

"I'm not sure about that. You do it all the time."

"Nonsense. Are you going to listen to me or not?"

"Let's hear it."

"They offered ten million. One payment upon signature."

Sebastian whistled.

"It's not that much for them, you know."

Sebastian realized he now was a millionaire. No, a multi-millionaire. That was more money than he had anticipated. However, he valued money as a way to get by. It was neither his goal nor his lifelong ambition. Still, he now had a lot of it. He kept quiet for a minute, thinking about his future.

"You don't have to work ever again. Travel the world in style." Uncle Mike had been thinking about the money, too.

He had never wanted the money, so it was not hard to stick with the decision he had reached already. "I know you said you'd do this pro bono, but I feel compelled to—"

"No, I forfeited my fees and I won't go back on my word."

"But you see, that is more money than I need. I have

a place to live. I have a job that is even paying for my move to Dallas."

"Hard to believe cheapskate Roger authorized that! I guess there goes your year-end bonus."

"Maybe. Anyway, what I want you to do is take the money and split it three ways. One third for me, one third for you. No, I don't want to hear it. You've earned it. The other third I want to give to James and Christine."

"Very generous of you."

"Pretty soon their kids will go to college, and they'll need it."

"Okay. I'm going to need their full names and bank account info."

"Come on, Uncle Mike! You're the big shot attorney who makes airlines write ten million dollar checks and you can't get one lousy doctor's bank info on your own?"

It didn't take long for Uncle Mike to digest the comment. "You won't tell them beforehand?"

"I won't give them the chance to say no," Sebastian said.

"Agree. Okay, I'll take care of it. When are you coming back to Dallas?"

"Need to do a couple of things. Like finish packing here. We made a garage sale of the furniture and I'm giving away other things. I'm bringing just my wardrobe and a few memories in a box."

"I understand you will be living at Bill's?"

"Yes. He called me in Honduras to say the apartment was still available."

"I think he called to see how you were doing."

"Nah, he wanted to close the deal." He laughed. In reality, he had spoken with Bill every day from hospital, and the apartment never came up until Sebastian asked for it.

He agreed to meet his uncle for dinner upon his return, then finished the conversation. He imagined James's face when he found the extra balance in his account. He figured some paperwork would need doing. A couple of million appearing out of the blue in a bank account would raise a few eyebrows in the IRS. After all, nothing in life is certain but death and taxes.

He summed up his recent accomplishments: apartment clean, clothes packed, his formal resignation to the FDNY sent, and his new money shared with his family.

Nothing left to do in New York.

It was time to move on.

ABOUT THE AUTHOR

J. H. Bográn, born and raised in Honduras, is the son of a journalist. Ironically, he prefers to write fiction rather than fact. His genre of choice is thrillers, but he likes to throw a twist of romance into the mix. His works include novels and short stories in both English and Spanish. He's a member of the Short Fiction Writers Guild and the International Thriller Writers where he also serves as the Thriller Roundtable Coordinator and contributing editor of their official e-zine *The Big Thrill*.

You can learn more on his website: *www.jhbogran.com* or follow him on Facebook at *www.facebook.com/jhbogran* and Twitter at @JHBogran.

Made in the USA
San Bernardino, CA
21 November 2013